WORLD FAMOUS MURDERS

Colin Wilson

Constable & Robinson Ltd
3 The Lanchesters
162 Fulham Palace Road
London W6 9ER

This edition published by Magpie Books,
an imprint of Constable & Robinson Ltd 2005

A copy of the British Library Cataloguing in Publication Data
is available from the British Library.

ISBN 1 84529 013 5

Printed and bound in the EU

Contents

Chapter One

The Mysterious Death of Justice Godfrey

The killing of Sir Edmund Berry Godfrey – in October 1678 – has been called the greatest murder mystery in English history. Its consequences were certainly appalling: a wave of hatred and violence unleashed against English Roman Catholics, resulting in more than twenty judicial murders and over a hundred imprisonments.

Godfrey was known as a decent and scrupulous man, courageous and rigidly honest. This is why his murder caused such widespread outrage among British Protestants, and why they allowed themselves to be persuaded that their Catholic countrymen were about to burn them all at the stake. The man whose sick imagination invented this 'Popish Plot' was a paranoid clergyman named Titus Oates, who is remembered as one of the most malevolent and vicious individuals in English history.

Edmund Berry Godfrey was born on 23 December 1621, the son of a Kentish gentleman of independent means. Educated at Westminster School and Christ Church, Oxford, he was prevented from entering his chosen profession, the law, by increasing deafness and ill health. His father solved the problem of a career by lending him £1,000 – worth about £40,000 in today's money – with which he and a friend named Harrison bought a wood wharf at Dowgate, near Thames Street in the City of London, and proceeded to sell wood and coal to their fellow Londoners. It was a good time to be in the fuel business. Winters were often so cold that the Thames froze solid. And the uncertainties of the Civil War between the Roundheads and the Royalists enabled them to charge high prices. By 1649, when King Charles lost his head, Godfrey and Harrison were already wealthy men. And the excitement of a business career had caused an enormous improvement in Godfrey's health. In 1658, when Godfrey took a house in Greens Lane, a road that ran between the Strand and the river (somewhere near present-day Villiers Street) he was the only coal merchant outside the city boundaries and had a kind of monopoly. In 1660, Godfrey followed in his father's footsteps by becoming a Justice of the Peace for Westminster and Middlesex.

He showed himself severe but fair minded. Harsh towards tramps and vagabonds, he was compassionate towards those whose misery and poverty were no fault of their own – in one case, he supported a family at a rate of ten pounds a year for several years until they were able to support themselves.

In the Great Plague of 1665, Godfrey was one of the few rich men who remained in London. This may not have been entirely a matter of altruism – in those days it was firmly believed that smoke could offer protection from the plague, and enormous fires were kept burning permanently in the streets, provided with fuel from Godfrey's coal and wood yard. Godfrey took charge of the digging of the largest mass grave in England – with plague deaths at £2,000 a week, individual burials had become impossible. Every night, carts drove through the streets, their drivers shouting 'bring out your dead'; blotched bodies, stinking of black vomit, were tossed onto the pile.

Godfrey himself seems to have had no fear of the plague. When he heard that a grave robber had taken refuge in a house full of plague victims, where the constables were afraid to follow him, he strode in with drawn sword and dragged the man out by the scruff of the neck. Later, the same man met him in the street and hurled himself on him with a heavy cudgel; Godfrey held him at bay with his sword until constables arrived to drag him away.

Since it was believed that dogs and cats spread the plague, thousands were exterminated. Nobody realized that the real culprit was the rats carrying the Bubonic Plague germ who bred in their thousands among the garbage that lay in London's streets. Fortunately, the winter that year was so cold that the plague slowly began to lose its grip. It was finally brought to an end by the Great Fire of London, which began in September 1666 and burned half the city in four days. Here again, Godfrey displayed his usual courage and industry, and soon after the end of the fire, King Charles II knighted him.

Three years later, Godfrey again revealed his courage in a conflict with the King. Alexander Frazier, one of the King's physicians, owed him thirty pounds for firewood – over £1,000 in modern money – and obviously had no intention of paying. As a member of the King's household, Frazier could not be taken to a court of law. Godfrey obtained a warrant from the sheriff and had Frazier arrested by bailiffs. The King was so enraged that he ordered the bailiffs to be whipped, but Godfrey ignored the King's command to have the warrant cancelled. Imprisoned in the porter's lodge at Whitehall, he went on hunger strike until, after six days, the King finally gave way. Fortunately, Charles was entirely lacking in vindictiveness, and bore Godfrey no grudge. It is not clear whether Godfrey ever received his thirty pounds.

And so, in his late forties, Godfrey was one of the most respected and well-loved figures in London. What strange twist of fate led him to become the victim of unknown murderers, less than ten years later?

Some weeks before his disappearance, Godfrey was

nervous, and it was clear that he expected to be killed. To one female acquaintance he remarked: 'Have you not heard that I am to be hanged?'

Yet if Godfrey *knew* he was going to be murdered, why did he not leave behind some clue that would bring the killers to justice? On the contrary, on the morning of his disappearance he burned all the papers that might have indicated who had killed him, and why.

On the morning of Saturday, 12 October 1678, Godfrey rose early and dressed in no less than three pairs of stockings – it was an icy cold day. When his housekeeper brought in his breakfast, Godfrey was talking to a man she did not recognize, who remained there for a long time. At eight o'clock he had left his house near Charing Cross, and walked up St Martin's Lane. Two acquaintances who said good morning noticed that he seemed to be withdrawn and depressed. In those days there were fields north of Oxford Street, and two hours later Godfrey was seen near the little village of Paddington. Then about an hour later, he was seen walking back through the muddy fields towards London. This must have been at about eleven o'clock in the morning.

Yet at about that same hour an acquaintance named Richard Adams called at Godfrey's house and was told by the servants: 'We have cause to fear Sir Edmund is made away.'

Sir Edmund had arranged to dine that day with a friend called Wynnel at a house not far from his home. When he failed to arrive by midday (which was the time they dined in the seventeenth century), Wynnel went to Godfrey's home, where the servants were looking upset and shaken. One of them told him: 'Ah Mr Wynnel, you will never see him more.'

Wynnel asked why. 'They say the Papists have been watching him for a long time, and that now they are very confident they have got him.'

Wynnel's efforts to extract further information were unsuccessful.

It seemed that Godfrey's brothers Michael and Benjamin, merchants in the City, had just received a message telling them that Sir Edmund had been murdered by Papists. They had hurried to his house and found that he'd left more than two hours before.

By two o'clock that afternoon it was rumoured all over London that Godfrey had been murdered by Papists.

That evening, he failed to return home. The following day his clerk went to Hammersmith, where Godfrey owned a tavern called the Swan, in King Street, but no one had seen him there.

The body was found the following Thursday, six days after his disappearance. At two o'clock in the afternoon, two men were walking through the fields of Primrose Hill – so called because it used to be covered in primroses. They were on their way to the White House Tavern in what is now Chalk Farm. As they passed a ditch, they noticed a cane, a belt and a pair of gloves lying on a green bank. Deciding that they probably belonged to some gentleman who was relieving himself in the bushes, they passed discreetly on. In the tavern, they told the landlord what they had seen, and he offered them a shilling if they would take him back to the place – he probably hoped for some profit in selling the items. They were still lying there. But as the landlord bent to pick them up, he saw a man lying face down in the ditch. A sword was sticking out between his shoulder blades.

The men gave the alarm to a local constable, and a dozen or so people made their way back to the body. The place was surrounded by bushes and brambles, which explained why it had not been seen earlier. The clothing revealed that this was obviously a gentleman – his periwig and hat lay a few feet away. As a number of men lifted the body out of

5

the ditch, someone commented, 'Pray God it be not Sir Edmund Berry Godfrey, for he hath for some time been missing.' The man who made the comment, Constable Brown, noted that, in spite of the sword that was driven right through the body, there was very little blood. He also noticed the curious fact that, although the fields were muddy – and had been so for many days – the corpse's shoes were quite clean. Obviously, he had not walked across the fields.

As they carried the body back to the tavern, the looseness of the neck seemed to suggest that it had been broken. And when it was laid out on a table, the blackened bruises which showed through the open doublet made it clear that the man had been violently beaten before death – perhaps kicked as he lay on the ground. Constable Brown, who knew Godfrey, had no doubt that the missing magistrate had been found. The next morning, when the body was more closely examined, the doctor noticed an odd clue: there were drops of candlewax on his breeches. But most people in those days did not use wax candles, which were expensive, but oil lamps. Even Godfrey's household did not use candles. Only priests used candles, commented a cleric who saw the body.

Priests . . . Again, it looked as if the Papists were responsible.

An inquest was later held on the body, and revealed that the stomach was completely empty. Since Godfrey had eaten breakfast shortly before he left home, this gave rise to a rumour that he had been held captive and starved for several days before his murder. In fact, the stomach takes only two or three hours to digest its food, and Godfrey had been walking long distances that morning.

Examination of the body suggested that death had been due to violent strangulation which had also broken the neck. The sword that had then been driven through the body was Godfrey's own. The fact that so little blood had emerged was probably because the sword plugged both the wounds in the front and the back.

At all events, it was obvious that Godfrey had died a particularly nasty and violent death. One obvious solution was that he'd been accosted by footpads or highwaymen – but this was contradicted by the fact that he had a great deal of money in his pockets – in fact, far more gold than a man would normally carry around loose. It was almost as if whoever had killed him had wished to indicate clearly that the motive was not robbery . . .

In the three centuries since the murder, many historians have propounded theories about who killed Justice Godfrey. Two obvious suspects are the men who originally found him – their names were Bromwell and Walters. They proved to be Catholics, and at one point during the investigation, were imprisoned for a short time as suspects. While they were in prison, there was an attempt to force them to admit that influential Catholics were involved in the murder, but they stuck to their story and were released. In retrospect, it seems obvious that, if they killed Godfrey, they had no reason to wait for six days before they 'found' the body.

The philosopher David Hume suggested that Godfrey had simply been killed by some criminal whom he had sent to prison at some point. But this fails to explain why Godfrey was so obviously worried for weeks before his murder.

A few years after the murder, Sir Roger L'Estrange, in *A Brief History of the Times*, suggested that Godfrey might have committed suicide. He was known to have been depressed for many weeks before his disappearance. One later suggestion was that he hanged himself, and that the body was found by Titus Oates, or one of his henchmen, and run through with Godfrey's own sword so that he appeared to have been murdered – thus provoking a backlash against Catholics. One writer even suggests that Godfrey was a sick man, and died of natural causes when he was in conference with the King and his brother the Duke of York, and that the 'murder' was an attempt by the King to avoid embarrassment. This seems highly unlikely since the Duke of York was a Catholic, the King was a secret Catholic, and Berry Godfrey was undoubtedly a staunch Protestant who, while he was not known to have any violent feelings against Catholics, was certainly not one of the 'King's party'. Finally, the novelist John Dickson Carr, in a fictional reconstruction of the case, suggested that Godfrey's two brothers may have been involved in the murder, since they seem to have been amongst the first to know about it. But Michael and Benjamin Godfrey claimed that they had been 'sent the information' on the morning their brother disappeared. If they were involved in the disappearance, why should they have hurried straight to his house and announced that they had heard he had been murdered?

In fact, if we look closely at the account of Godfrey's disappearance – even in the brief version presented above – certain facts stand out very clearly. Let us imagine that these facts have been placed in front of Sherlock Holmes.

The first thing Holmes notes is that Godfrey believed he was going to be murdered for some considerable time before it happened. That implied that he knew the identity of the killer or killers. This meant that, if there was a 'plot' behind his death, then Godfrey himself must have been involved in it in some way. The plotters were friends, or at least acquaintances. And Godfrey had his reasons for not wishing to betray them.

On the day before his disappearance, an unknown messenger called at Godfrey's home. He carried a letter tied with string. The housekeeper took the letter in to Godfrey, and after he had read it, told him that the messenger was waiting for an answer. Godfrey was looking puzzled. 'Pr'ythee, tell him I don't know what to make of it.'

Titus Oates

Murders

Later that same evening, after a meeting of the vestry, Godfrey realized that a man called Bradbury had been wrongly fined two pounds. When Godfrey got home, he sent for Bradbury, and returned the two pounds to him. When a friend commented on this, Godfrey said: 'I am resolved to settle all my business tonight . . .' All this suggests that he knew that death was breathing down his neck.

The fact that Godfrey was battered – probably kicked in the ribs when he was on the ground – then strangled with enough violence to break his neck, then run through with his own sword suggests conspirators who had a considerable grudge against him. Such a grudge suggests that they believed that Godfrey had betrayed them in some way. Who were these conspirators?

The obvious answer that presents itself is that they were something to do with Titus Oates and his 'Popish Plot'. Godfrey's murder was used to stir up anti-Catholic feeling, and to justify a Catholic persecution not unlike Hitler's persecution of the Jews in the twentieth century. Titus Oates was, in effect, the Himmler in charge of this persecution.

So let us assume, merely as a plausible theory, that Titus Oates and his gang of anti-Catholic conspirators were behind the murder. Let us suppose that they deliberately chose Justice Godfrey because he was known as an honest man and widely respected and admired. Is it not possible that Godfrey was murdered simply because his death would provoke widespread outrage?

There is one obvious objection to this. Godfrey knew in advance that he was going to be murdered. If he guessed that he was to be killed merely to provoke anti-Catholic feeling, why did he not tell people, and make quite sure the suspicion fell on Titus Oates?

It is time to look a little more closely at Titus Oates and the history of the Popish Plot.

The first 'Locked Room Mystery' was Poe's
'Murders in the Rue Morgue'. The first locked room
novel seems to have been John Ratcliffe's *Neno Sahib*.
This inspired a real murder. In 1881, the wife and five
children of a Berlin carter named Fritz Conrad were
found hanging from hooks in a locked room. It
looked as if Frau Conrad, depressed by poverty, had
killed her children and committed suicide. Police
Commissioner Hollman was suspicious, and when
he found out that Conrad was infatuated with a
young girl student, he searched the apartment for
love letters. He found none, but came upon a copy of
Neno Sahib and read Ratcliffe's account of a 'perfect
murder', in which the killer drilled a tiny hole in the
door, passed a thread through it, and used this to
draw the bolt after the murder; he then sealed up
the hole with wax. Hollman examined Conrad's
door, and found a similar hole, filled in with sealing
wax, to which threads of horsehair still adhered.
Confronted with this evidence, Conrad confessed to
murdering his wife and children, and was sentenced
to death.

Oates, born in 1649 at Oakham in Rutland, was an
unpleasant child, whose father called him 'Snotty Fool' and
whose schoolfellows knew him as 'Filthy Mouth'. He was
bow-legged, ugly and accustomed to being disliked. In
addition, he was homosexual, in a time when homosexuality
was a capital crime. He must have felt resentful against a fate
that had endowed him with an inclination that he was unable
to satisfy without risking his life.

After a year at Merchant-Taylors School in London, he

was expelled for unknown reasons. When he was eighteen, he spent two terms at Caius College, Cambridge, but was thrown out – probably because he was such a spectacularly bad student – in 1668. He managed to get himself admitted to St John's College in the following year, but after tricking a poor tailor out of a coat, he was sent down in disgrace.

Somehow, he managed to get himself ordained as a curate after obtaining the favour of the Catholic Earl of Norwich. There he later claimed to hear the first rumours of a plot by England's Roman Catholics to rise up against the Protestants.

England, of course, had been Protestant since Henry VIII's break with Rome in 1533. 'Bloody Mary's attempt to restore Catholicism by burning hundreds of 'heretics' gave the English a real reason to hate Rome, and Foxe's *Book of Martyrs* kept the memory of the horrors alive. In fact, the English were not really a religiously minded people – the historian Conyers Read observed that 'in thirty years they accepted five distinct changes in their religion without any great fuss about the matter'. That is why they reacted so strongly against religious fanatics like Mary. Charles I was not actually a Catholic, but he was a kind of crypto-Catholic – that is, a High Anglican who detested Puritanism, and whose fervent belief in God was based upon the conviction that God had appointed him to rule England. His Parliament disagreed, as a result of which Charles lost his head.

By the time of Charles II, the common people of England had no particular hatred of Catholicism, but they were determined not to have it imposed on them by force. Charles was rightly suspected of being a secret Catholic, and the conversion of his brother James was an open secret at least ten years before the murder of Sir Edmund Berry Godfrey. His views about the privileges of royalty were as strong and as unrealistic as those of his father – which explains why, when he became king, his reign lasted only three years. Charles, who was altogether more flexible and adaptable, succeeded in staying on the throne for twenty-five years.

Even so, there were several attempts to unseat him. In 1661, a religious fanatic called Thomas Venner plunged London into chaos for three days as his armour-clad followers attempted to inaugurate the millennium. He was finally defeated by the army, and executed with twelve of his lieutenants.

In the following year, a man called Thomas Tonge planned to ambush and murder the King. It was discovered and he was also executed. In 1663, there was a Yorkshire Plot led by Colonel Thomas Blood (later famous for trying to steal the Crown Jewels) and a captain called Oates (no relation of Titus). It was infiltrated by government agents and Oates and twenty other conspiritors were executed. In 1666, Colonel John Rathbone plotted to kill the King, set fire to London, and turn England into a Republic. He also ended hanging from Tyburn tree.

In 1670, Charles entered into a secret treaty with 'the Sun King', Louis XIV of France. In return, he received £140,000 from Louis. The first step towards fulfilling his promise of cooperation was a Declaration of Indulgence, allowing Catholics to worship in private houses without danger of arrest. But there were still many followers of Oliver Cromwell who regarded this as the thin end of the wedge, another attempt to impose Catholicism on England by force. The Declaration of Indulgence aroused so much opposition that Charles was soon forced to withdraw it.

One of the most violent anti-Catholics in England was the Earl of Shaftesbury, who had changed sides in the Civil War and fought for Cromwell. But he opposed Cromwell in Parliament, and was one of those who were instrumental in bringing Charles back to England after Cromwell's death. Shaftesbury was outraged when he found out about Charles's secret treaty with Louis XIV, and he supported a Test Act directed against Catholics, which would force them to come into the open by forswearing their religion. (It forced Charles's brother James to resign various offices that he held.) Shaftesbury was made to resign. He appointed himself leader of the Opposition and became in effect the first party political leader in English history. The secret aim of most of the Opposition was to get rid of the King and restore a republic.

Shaftesbury became friendly with all the extremist Protestants in Parliament, and persuaded many of them to join a group that he called the Green Ribbon Club, which met at the King's Head tavern in Fleet Street. Its president was a man called Sir Robert Peyton, and in October 1677, Peyton and his 'Gang' plotted to attack the Tower of London, kill the King and the Duke of York, and set up Richard Cromwell, son of Oliver Cromwell, as the ruler of England. But the King's spy network was too much for them. When they realized that their plot was known to the King, they hastily abandoned it. And because so many of the plotters were influential men, they were never called to account.

During these years, Titus Oates had been getting himself into trouble as a drunkard and a thief. Dismissed by the Archbishop of Canterbury, he became his father's curate, and was soon accusing a local schoolmaster of buggering a child in the front porch of the church. Oates also accused the schoolmaster's father of treasonable speeches. When these cases were dismissed, and it became obvious that Titus Oates was a perjurer, he fled.

He went to sea as a naval chaplain, but even the Royal Navy found his enthusiasm for sodomising young sailors excessive, and he came close to being hanged, after which he was drummed out of the navy.

The Mysterious Death of Justice Godfrey

In London in 1677, he met another rabid anti-Catholic called Dr Israel Tonge, an ardent ex-Puritan who had lost his job at Oxford with the return of King Charles. Now, with the aid of anti-Catholics, Tonge has become vicar of St Mary Stayning in the City of London. But his church was destroyed in the Great Fire, and in his misery, Tonge became convinced that the Great Fire had been started by Catholics, as a first step towards re-converting England. He became a totally obsessed crank, pouring his venom into the ear of anybody who would listen. Titus Oates was one of the few who was not only ready to listen, but to contribute his own poisonous fantasies.

Quite simply, Titus Oates wanted power. He felt that the age owed him a living, and that any means were allowable to persuade people to entrust him with power.

It seems that Tonge's willingness to accept the worst slanders against Catholics inspired Oates with the Popish Plot. He told Tonge that he had evidence that Catholics all over England were preparing to rebel, murder the King, and then slaughter all the Protestants. It was all inspired by the Pope, who had ordered the Jesuits to kill King Charles and replace him with his brother James. On 12 August 1678 – two months before Godfrey's murder – another anti-Catholic crank called Christopher Kirkby, a London merchant, called on Tonge at his house in the Barbican, and was told the dreadful secret. Tonge showed him an enormous pile of papers which, he claimed, proved the existence of the Plot. Soon, said Tonge, Louis XIV was going to land in Ireland, and King Charles's physician was going to poison the King.

Kirkby was a man of action. He declared that the King had to be informed immediately. So he wrote a letter, waited outside Whitehall Palace until the King came by with a group of courtiers, and then rushed forward and pressed the letter into his hand. The King opened it and read it. He was obviously impressed. He asked Kirkby to wait for him in the palace, and later questioned him fully about the 'Plot'. Later on, he met with Kirkby and Tonge, and Tonge handed over a copy of the long and involved account of the Plot written by Titus Oates. According to Oates, the King was going to be assassinated by two Catholics called Pickering and Grove. They had made several attempts to kill him over the course of eight years, but been unable to get close enough. Now they were going to make another attempt with the aid of 'four Irish ruffians'.

The King was a shrewd enough judge of character to realize that Kirkby and Tonge were cranks. But it would obviously be stupid not to look into the matter. So he passed the investigation into the hands of his treasurer, the Earl of Danby.

Tonge said that a friend of his called Lloyd was in touch with the assassins. He would persuade them to take the stagecoach to Windsor, and the King's men would be waiting there to arrest them. But when the coach arrived, only Lloyd was in it. He explained that some accident had prevented the assassins from taking the coach. A few days later, yet another attempt to arrest the assassins ended in failure – Tonge said that one of their horses had fallen down and injured its shoulder. By this time, Danby was fairly certain that the whole thing was pure invention. The King himself now began to feel that Tonge and Kirkby were mere attention-seekers.

Now desperate, Titus Oates forged a number of letters that were supposed to have been written to James's confessor, the Jesuit Father Bedingfield. These, according to Tonge, were full of treasonable material that would prove the existence of the plot. Danby arranged to have the letters intercepted, but something went wrong, and they got through to Bedingfield. He realized that somebody was trying to 'frame' him and took them straight to James, who in turn took them straight to the King.

So now Titus Oates was desperate. His Popish Plot was simply falling apart. If he was going to avoid landing in jail, he had to think of something new.

At this point, just as the Plot was about to collapse for lack of support, James came to the rescue. Far less intelligent than his brother the King, he failed to realize that the best thing he could do was to ignore it. He pressed for a much fuller investigation.

The investigator Danby decided that the next step would be to get Oates to swear to his various accusations on oath. One London magistrate flatly declined to have anything to do with it. Justice Godfrey was rash enough – or perhaps innocent enough – to agree to do it. So at the end of September, Oates and Tonge arrived at Godfrey's house, presented him with two copies of Oates's absurd rigmarole, and Godfrey made Oates take the oath and then countersigned the papers.

In effect, the highly respected Justice Godfrey was being used to lend credibility to the paranoid fantasies of Titus Oates.

Events moved swiftly. That same day, Tonge and Kirkby were summoned to the Council Chamber in Whitehall for a meeting of the Privy Council. The King sat at the head of the table, and the men who surrounded it were all princes, dukes or earls. The Secretary of State, Sir Joseph Williamson, told the Council that they were there to consider information about a Jesuit conspiracy against the life of His Majesty. This caused a sensation. Then Charles described how he had first met with Kirkby and Tonge, and also told them about the forged letters to Bedingfield.

Charles was obviously bored with the whole affair, but the councillors were all new to the Plot, and listened with fascination. Tonge and Kirkby were closely questioned, and they managed to sound convincing.

Finally Titus Oates himself was called. No one knows

quite what the Council thought when they saw this bow-legged man with a bright red face and bulging eyes, but they were certainly impressed when Oates asked whether he could begin by taking the oath. After that, he launched into details of the Popish Plot, which the Council had just been reading about. When showed the forged letters, he claimed that he recognized the handwriting in them to be that of various Jesuit conspirators. Oates proved to be an impressive witness, with the ability to convince and persuade. Before the evening was over, the Council had issued warrants of arrest for various conspirators including Grove and Pickering, and of various Jesuits. When Oates left the chamber, he walked with his head upright; he had ceased to be a despised nobody, and turned into a man who was in a position to take his revenge upon his enemies. That night, he and his men dragged several Jesuits from their beds and marched them off to Newgate Prison.

The only person who was not convinced was the King. He had done his best to show that Oates was a liar. When Oates said he had met Don John of Austria, the King asked him what Don John looked like. 'A tall man,' said Oates and the King replied: 'Wrong, he is short.' But Oates was unabashed, and replied that he had been told that the man was Don John, and that was all he knew about it.

The next night, armed with more warrants, Oates and his friends arrested twenty or so more Jesuits.

By this time Sir Edmund Berry Godfrey had had time to read the papers thoroughly, and become convinced that Oates was a liar. He was thrown into doubt and confusion. He himself was a Protestant. If he denounced the Popish Plot as the paranoid fantasy of a maniac, it would probably delight James and his fellow Catholics, but would cause his fellow Protestants to regard him as a traitor.

This is why, two weeks before his murder, Sir Edmund Berry Godfrey became a deeply troubled man.

The Mysterious Death of Justice Godfrey

And so came the day when a mysterious messenger delivered a letter to Godfrey, and Godfrey told his housekeeper: 'Tell him I don't know what to make of it.' But when he left his home the next day, he obviously had a strong suspicion that this was to be the last day of his life.

What exactly happened? How did this honest and decent man come to fear for his life? Why did he choose to shield the people he suspected were planning to murder him?

For more than three centuries after the murder of Sir Edmund Berry Godfrey these questions remained unanswered. And it was about this time – in 1978 – that a young journalist named Stephen Knight who had just written a book called *Jack the Ripper: the Final Solution* (1976) decided to return to the problem that had intrigued him since he was a teenager: the murder of Sir Edmund Berry Godfrey. It was his modest ambition simply to present the most historically accurate account of the case on record. But as he studied papers in the Public Record Office, the British Museum and various university libraries, he suddenly realized with astonishment that he had finally solved the mystery.

'The remarkable truth, never before disclosed, is that Sir Edmund Berry Godfrey was one of those Republican conspirators dedicated to the overthrow of Charles and the setting up of [Richard] Cromwell.' In other words, Godfrey was a member of 'Peyton's Gang', the group of 'Green Ribbon' conspirators who had planned to murder Charles, seize the Tower of London and set up Richard Cromwell as dictator in 1677. This plot, as we have already noted, had been foiled by the King's spies, but the people involved – including the Earl of Shaftesbury – were all so powerful that, without absolutely conclusive evidence, they were virtually untouchable.

Knight established beyond doubt that Sir Edmund Berry Godfrey was a member of 'Peyton's Gang'. Half of the Gang had, in fact, been stripped of their public offices. But there was nothing positive against Godfrey, and in any case, he was not a part of the government.

Knight found the first indication of Godfrey's involvement in the secret papers of Sir Joseph Williamson, the Secretary of State – a list of names of the twelve members of 'Peyton's Gang', in which Sir Edmund Berry Godfrey is number four.

The next piece of evidence was a letter, dated 1674, describing a meeting of anti-Catholic members of Parliament at the 'Swan tavern in King Streete'. But the Swan tavern in King Street in Hammersmith belonged to Sir Edmund Berry Godfrey.

When half of Peyton's Gang were 'purged' in 1677, Godfrey must have known that he was walking a tightrope. The King already had reason to dislike him for the attempt to arrest his physician for debt. Now it was necessary for him to tread with extreme care. This is probably why he agreed to take the oath of Oates and Tonge – an event that proved to be the turning point in the success of the Popish Plot. He did not dare to have his loyalty questioned.

All this explains why Godfrey was worried in case the King signed a warrant for his arrest. But why should he be worried that his fellow conspirators should regard him as a traitor?

It is at this point that we come upon one of those strange twists in the plot that would defy even the deductive powers of Sherlock Holmes. As incredible as it sounds, the Earl of Shaftesbury, that dedicated anti-Catholic, was also taking money from the King of France, Louis XIV. And why *should* Louis want to encourage anti-Catholic opposition in England? There was a perfectly straightforward and cynical reason. Louis had deliberately set out to make himself the most powerful ruler in Europe. England was the traditional enemy of the French, and even with Charles II on the throne, Louis could never be sure that England would not decide to try and thwart his designs. (In fact, when William of Orange forced James II to flee, and became King of England in 1689, this is precisely what happened – England joined with Holland, Sweden and Spain, and wrecked Louis's plan of becoming master of The Netherlands.) It was in Louis's interest to keep England as weak as possible, and the best way of doing this was to stir up civil unrest so that the King had more than enough problems on his hands. This is why he became the secret paymaster of the King's enemies.

Now it so happened that the man who carried the money from Louis to Shaftesbury's Opposition was a strange, dreamy Catholic visionary named Edward Coleman, who had been secretary to the King's brother James, and was now secretary to James's wife the Duchess of York. And for some extraordinary reason that even Stephen Knight was unable to uncover, Edward Coleman was also a friend of Sir Edmund Berry Godfrey. There is no obvious reason why the two should be friends. But then in spite of his desire to see England turned again into a republic, Godfrey seems to have been a reasonable, friendly kind of man, and it is simply possible that he had met Coleman in the course of his duties as a magistrate or a vestryman, and taken a deep liking to him.

This was the real cause of Sir Edmund Berry Godfrey's downfall.

Titus Oates included Coleman's name in the list of Jesuit plotters. When Godfrey discovered his name in the papers of Titus Oates, he immediately warned Coleman. The result was that Coleman burned most of his private papers and fled. Oates and his gang arrived shortly afterwards, and tore the house to pieces. Unfortunately, Coleman had forgotten an old wooden box full of papers hidden in a secret recess behind one of the chimneys.

Among these were letters in which Coleman – who was a Catholic convert – spoke wistfully about his dreams of seeing James on the throne and England once again converted to Catholicism. Coleman was not actually a plotter, but once Titus Oates had whipped anti-Catholic fever up into a fury that recalls the anti-communist purges of Senator Joseph McCarthy, it was easy to see these letters as proof of the Popish Plot. Coleman was arrested, dragged to the King's Bench bar that November – after the death of Godfrey – and sentenced to death, one of more than 200 innocent Catholics to lose their lives as a result of Oates's malevolence.

In all probability, Oates had somehow got wind of the fact that Coleman was a friend of Godfrey's. Coleman's name was inserted into the papers at a fairly late date – as if to deliberately test Godfrey's loyalty. And although Coleman took the trouble to change his identity to 'Mr Clarke' when he went to meet Godfrey at the house of his friend Colonel Welden, Oates's spies undoubtedly knew precisely what had happened.

During those first two weeks of October, Godfrey realized that his past had caught up with him. He had done his best to be a decent and honourable citizen, and to offend no one. But he *had* allowed his Protestant sympathies to draw him into association with Shaftesbury and the Green Ribboners. Now he knew that he was going to be asked to pay the price.

On that afternoon before his death, when the mysterious messenger came with a letter, Godfrey was undoubtedly summoned to appear in front of his 'honourable friends' to explain himself. He undoubtedly hoped that his explanations would satisfy them, and they would cease to entertain any doubt of his loyalty. What he may not have known is that many of these 'honourable friends' were entirely in favour of Oates and his Popish Plot. He certainly failed to realize that his own murder would be the best piece of anti-Catholic propaganda that Oates could hope for.

What was it in the letter that made him say to his house-keeper: 'Pr'ythee, tell him I don't know what to make of it'? As Knight points out, there can surely be only one answer. For some reason, the letter asked him to bring a large quantity of gold. Why should the conspirators tell him to bring gold with him? The answer, of course, was that when he was found murdered, the presence of the gold in his pockets would make it quite clear that he had not been killed by footpads or highwaymen. The finger would point straight at the Catholics.

That day, Godfrey kept his appointment, some time around the middle of the day. Yet his brothers had already been told that he was murdered. The intention was to cause maximum scandal.

Stephen Knight believes that he even knows the identity of the man who killed him. One of the gang of violent anti-Catholics was a murderous giant called Philip Herbert, the seventh Earl of Pembroke. He died of alcoholism at the age of thirty, but in the meantime showed himself to be a man whose violence amounted to a form of insanity. His sister-in-law, the Duchess of Portsmouth, was the King's favourite mistress. He took his seat in the House of Lords in 1675, when he was eighteen, and was soon appointed Lord Lieutenant of Wiltshire. Although recently married, he neglected his wife and spent most of his time in debauchery. He surrounded himself with wild animals – fifty-two mastiffs, thirty greyhounds, some bears and a lion, as well as 'sixty fellowes more bestial than they'.

Typical of his violence was an affray that happened when he had invited a jury to drink in a tavern. Everyone was afraid to sit next to him until Sir Francis Vincent took the empty seat. When Sir Francis declined to pledge a toast, Pembroke seized a full bottle and broke it over his head. The injured Sir Francis was being taken to his coach when he was told that Pembroke was following him with his sword drawn. Sir Francis stood his ground, and Pembroke tried to strike him so violently that he broke his sword. Vincent threw away his own sword and attacked Pembroke so fiercely that he knocked him unconscious. Vincent then found himself pursued by some of Pembroke's thugs, but managed to throw one of them in the Thames, and fight off the others with the aid of some redcoats who arrived.

One evening, Pembroke saw a curtained sedan chair being carried through St James's Park and shouted drunkenly: 'Who's there?' The man inside answered non-committally, at which Pembroke shouted: 'Whoever you are, I will kill you' and drove his sword through the draperies, just missing the nose of the man inside. This is the kind of thing that Pembroke frequently did on impulse.

Once, when Pembroke was about to lose a duel one of his thugs slashed at his opponent and cut his hand. As the opponent staggered back, Pembroke drove his sword into his belly.

On Christmas Day 1677, Pembroke grabbed a parson and insisted that they should get drunk together. The minister was forced to drink three large glasses of sack [sherry] while he listened to 'outrageous blasphemies against our blessed Lord and the Virgin Mother'. This time, Pembroke was thrown into the Tower for blasphemy. But a few weeks later, the House of Lords issued a warrant for his release on the grounds that only the clergyman had borne witness against him. A few days later, a gentleman of Kent called Philip Ricaut was standing at the door of a friend's house in the Strand when, without provocation, Pembroke hit him violently in the eye, and then knocked him to the ground and jumped on him, almost choking him to death. Pembroke drew his sword and was about to thrust through

Ricaut when the latter managed to scramble into his friend's house and slam the door.

Soon after this, Pembroke became involved in a drunken quarrel with a man called Nathaniel Cony – on some minor provocation – and kicked and trampled upon him so violently that Cony died of his injuries. Stephen Knight notes that these injuries are similar to those found on Sir Edmund Berry Godfrey. This time, Pembroke was sentenced to death. But he pleaded benefit of clergy – which at that time merely meant that he could read and write. So the sentence was suspended, and although all his lands were forfeited to the Crown, they were restored to him by the King's warrant two days later.

Knight cites a number of other cases in which the 'Mad Peer' committed murder and got away with it. On the whole, his argument that it was Pembroke who was selected to murder Sir Edmund Berry Godfrey is convincing.

In the pogrom that followed Godfrey's death, Titus Oates had a free hand. All Catholics – and other dissenters – were ordered to depart ten miles from London. Meanwhile, Catholics were arrested every day, accused of whatever came into Titus Oates's head, and usually executed, very often by being hanged, drawn and quartered at Tyburn.

Typical of the methods of Titus Oates was his attempt to cause the downfall of Samuel Pepys, the Secretary of the Navy, and a close friend of the King's brother James. One of Pepys's clerks, Samuel Atkins, was arrested and taken before the Lord's Committee. A certain Captain Atkins, a member of Shaftesbury's Gang, alleged that Samuel Atkins (no relation) had told him that Pepys hated Sir Edmund Berry Godfrey, and 'would be the ruin of him'. According to Captain Atkins, the clerk had asked him about a seaman named Child, and asked him to send Child to see Pepys. Later, claimed Captain Atkins, he saw Child, and the seaman told him that Pepys had tried to persuade him to join in 'the murder of a man'.

Samuel Atkins, with transparent honesty, denied all this. He also declared that he had never seen Captain Atkins in his life. When Atkins repeated his perjuries in front of him, Samuel Atkins said, 'God, your conscience and I know it is notoriously untrue.' He was thrown into Newgate, and resisted all attempts to persuade him to save his neck by betraying his master. Fortunately, Oates was so busy perjuring himself about other Catholics that Atkins was forgotten and finally released.

Three Catholics named Green, Berry and Hill were indicted for Godfrey's murder. They were undoubtedly innocent, but Oates obtained his evidence against them by the same method that he had tried to use against Samuel Pepys. A Catholic named Miles Prance was indiscreet enough to declare in a coffee house that he thought that some of the 'Popish Plotters' were 'honest men'. He was arrested, and accused of being involved in the murder of Justice Godfrey. Like Samuel Atkins, he was thrown into Newgate. Realizing that he would probably end on the gallows, he finally sent a message to the Lord's Committee promising to give information. In front of the Committee, he claimed that he had seen Godfrey being followed continually by Green and Hill on the morning of his disappearance. The whole story was manifestly an invention, but it served the purpose of the anti-Catholics, and the three men were found guilty and hanged.

It has been estimated that there were thirty-five judicial murders as a result of Oates's perjuries. But in July 1679, some of his lies were exposed at the trial of the Queen's doctor, Wakeman, and the judge directed the jury to acquit. Oates succeeded in whipping up public frenzy against the judge, but nevertheless, the pace of the terror slowed. Charles fought ferociously to prevent his brother from

The great American *cause célèbre* of 1904 was the trial of *Floradora* girl Nan Patterson for the murder of her lover Caesar Young in a hansom cab. The shot that killed gambler Caesar Young was fired at about eight o'clock on the morning of 4 June 1904; he was dead by the time he reached hospital. Nan Patterson claimed he committed suicide but the police disbelieved her – to begin with, the revolver was in Young's pocket, and it seemed unlikely he would have placed it there after shooting himself.

Young, who was married; had met Nan Patterson on a train to California two years earlier. It was a passionate affair, but by 1904, Young wanted to terminate it; to that end he booked passage to Europe for himself and his wife on the *Germanic*. He and Nan spent a last evening quarrelling violently. He nevertheless met her for a breakfast of brandy and whisky, after which they called the hansom, and Young was shot soon after. Under the circumstances, Nan's story that he killed himself because he was upset about leaving her seemed unlikely – the bullet had entered at the wrong angle. At her first trial, a juror became ill, so a mistrial was declared. Her second trial ended with a hung jury. When the third trial also ended in deadlock, all charges against her were dropped. In retrospect it seems clear that Nan was acquitted, not because she was innocent, but because the men on the jury felt she was too pretty to hang.

Nan cashed in her notoriety by accepting leading roles in various musicals, but proved to lack talent, and soon vanished into obscurity.

being excluded from the throne. Finally, Charles won, and for the last four years of his reign, Shaftesbury's influence was broken. Titus Oates had become an irrelevance. In 1682 Oates's pension was reduced and then stopped, and he was forbidden to come to court. In 1684 he was charged with having called James a traitor, and fined £100,000 in damages. When James came to the throne in 1685, Oates was finally tried and convicted for perjury. Judge Jeffreys imposed a barbarous sentence, which included two whippings, five appearances in the pillory every year, and life imprisonment. The whippings almost killed Oates, but he survived. He spent the three years of James's reign in Newgate, where he succeeded in impregnating one of the prison bedmakers. When James was forced to flee, and William of Orange came to the throne, he was released and given a small pension. In 1698 the government actually gave him £500 to pay his debts. He became a Baptist preacher in Wapping, but was expelled for 'disorderly conduct and hypocrisy'. He died in 1705.

Chapter Two

What Happened to Jimmy Hoffa?

The disappearance of Teamsters' Union leader Jimmy Hoffa can hardly be described as one of the great mysteries of our time, there can be very little doubt of what happened to him and why it happened. But as a piece of criminal – and social – history, there can be no doubt that it ranks as one of the most fascinating stories of the twentieth century.

This story has to begin a long way back, at the end of the American Civil War in 1865.

Like all wars, this one had been a tremendous boost to industry, and America's Industrial Revolution began immediately after the war. Civil War General Ulysses Grant was elected president, and Grant believed that national prosperity depended on Big Business. The result was that massive fortunes were made overnight by men who were little more than large-scale buccaneers and pirates. Commodore Cornelius Vanderbilt told his critics, 'What do I care about the law? Ain't I got the power?' Every other day, Wall Street witnessed crooked deals that would now earn a man a lifetime in jail. A young pirate named Jim Fisk combined with an equally unscrupulous man called Jay Gould to swindle the $19,000,000 Erie Railroad from Fisk's patron Daniel Drew, then they bought a printing press and printed enough new Erie stock certificates to raise the Railroad's value to $57,000,000. The son of an itinerant medicine peddler named John D. Rockefeller succeeded in starting a small company called Standard Oil in Ohio, which swiftly achieved a monopoly of oil refining throughout the United States. Rockefeller was a Baptist Sunday School teacher of sober habits, but most of his fellow robber barons were men with a taste for big cigars and expensive mistresses. In 1872, Jim Fisk was shot to death by patrician Ned Stokes, the latest lover of Fisk's mistress Josie Mansfield. Boss William Tweed caught the spirit of the times when he became Tammany boss in New York, and swindled the city out of $30,000,000, by such expedients as charging the city $482,500 for safes valued at $3,450. Tweed got caught and sent to prison, but dozens like him flourished under the protection of President Grant.

The only people who failed to profit from the bonanza were the workers. Good capitalist principles meant that they were paid a minimum wage, often as little as ten cents an hour, and fired if they showed any sign of wanting a raise. At the age of fourteen, Jack London once worked continually for thirty-six hours without a break and was paid four dollars. Later, he got a job shovelling coal at the power plant of the Oakland Street railway, and set out to gain promotion. He found it impossible to believe that human beings could be expected to work so hard for thirty dollars a month on both the day and night shifts. One day he discovered that he had been doing the work of two men, both of whom had been paid forty dollars a month; the superintendent had got rid of one of them when he discovered that London would work so hard, and pocketed the fifty dollars himself. One of the men whose job London had taken had committed suicide because his family were starving.

This kind of thing caused understandable militancy, and it was increased by the periodic depressions that brought millions of people close to starvation. Labour leaders like Eugene Debs organized the workers into unions, and

What Happened to Jimmy Hoffa?

Teamster leader Jimmy Hoffa

pulled them out on strike. In the *année terrible* 1894, three-quarters of a million working men came out on strike. The bosses often retaliated by hiring strike breakers, many of whom were thugs and ex-convicts. Some bosses formed an alliance with the Mafia, and strike leaders were often beaten up or killed.

This was the situation when James Riddle Hoffa was born into a working-class Pennsylvania Dutch-Irish family in February 1913 in Indiana. The family was fairly prosperous until the father, a coal prospector, died in 1920. After that his wife took in laundry and worked as a cleaning woman to feed her family.

Jimmy left school in 1927, when he was fourteen, and went to work at twelve dollars a week for a sixty-hour week. In 1929, he found a job unloading railroad cars that carried food for the city of Detroit, where the family had moved. The pay seemed excellent – thirty-two cents an hour – until Hoffa found out that there was a catch. They were only paid for the time they were unloading the boxcars. But they might sit around idle for half the day. A bullying foreman made the job even more intolerable.

Together with two more workers, Hoffa organized a sit-down strike on a day when a shipment of strawberries came in. In less than an hour the employer – the grocery chain Krogers – surrendered, realizing that they were going to lose thousands of dollars' worth of strawberries. They signed a contract that gave the men a thirteen cent an hour pay rise, a guaranteed half day of work each day, and recognition of their union.

Within a year, Hoffa was working full time for the International Brotherhood of Teamsters. The union spread. When some of the bosses hired Mafia gangsters to intimidate the union men, Hoffa organized his own men to fight back with baseball bats.

But Hoffa also took the first step on the downward path

that would lead to his destruction. He approached the Detroit Purple Gang, a Jewish Mafia, and hired them to fight back. The tactic was effective, but Hoffa would later learn that there were heavy unseen costs.

In one year, Hoffa was beaten up repeatedly, and had to have his scalp stitched up six times. On one occasion he was kicked to the ground and stamped on. As he was losing consciousness, one of the 'goons' snarled in his ear: 'This is only a sample. Next time you're dead.'

But this short, powerfully built man refused to be intimidated. The more the workers had to fight strike breakers, the stronger their sense of fellowship became. By the time he was twenty-four, Hoffa was the head of one of the most powerful unions in America. In that same year, 1937, he organized the Teamsters of Detroit to stage a city-wide strike for higher wages and better working conditions. Three days later the trucking companies gave way.

But once again, Hoffa had been forced to compromise. Before the strike began, he approached members of Detroit's Mafia underworld, and somehow persuaded them not to intervene. How he persuaded them is uncertain.

In 1941, Hoffa again showed his organizing skills in getting rid of the communists in the Minneapolis branch. The communists were further left than Hoffa's Teamsters, and they were thinking of taking their own members into a rival organization, the CIO (Congress of Industrial Organizations). Hoffa got rid of them with his usual strong-arm tactics – baseball bats and car tyre chains. Then he carried the battle to the CIO in Detroit. During the struggle, the citizens of Detroit got used to the spectacle of rival unionists fighting one another in the streets like gangsters competing for territory.

It was during this inter-union war against the rich and powerful CIO that Hoffa once again decided he needed allies. Again, it was the Mafia who helped him to fight the

CIO. After innumerable beatings and killings, the CIO decided to leave Detroit to Hoffa and his Teamsters. But Hoffa owed his victory to 'the mob'.

Hoffa was by now a happily married man with two children. He also had a kind of stepson – Chuckie O'Brien, the son of Sylvia Pigano, a woman he had once wanted to marry. Chuckie spent long periods with the Hoffas.

Another honorary family member was Sylvia Pigano's boyfriend, Tony Giacalone, a Detroit gangster. Hoffa, who was deeply loyal to his friends, trusted him completely.

Inevitably, Hoffa became involved in his own forms of illegality. Since his Teamsters constituted a kind of monopoly, he was able to force grocers who used non-union trucks to pay heavy 'protection'. In 1946 these activities caught up with him and he appeared in court. He was let off with a fine and a caution.

By this time he was president of the Detroit Local 299, and head of a joint council for the Detroit area. As the chairman of the Central States Drivers Council he was able to extend his influence to the South, forcing trucking companies to employ union men. Little by little, he was adding to his empire.

When Teamster president Dan Tobin stepped down in 1952, he was replaced by Dave Beck, who treated Hoffa as his right-hand man. Now Hoffa was getting very close to the top.

He decided to move east, to New York. When the Teamsters there rebuffed him, Hoffa hired gangsters to set up local unions which existed only on paper, but which gave them a vote and enabled Hoffa to take over the New York Teamsters.

One of these new East Teamsters was a member of the Vito Genovese mob, Tony Provenzano, known as 'Tony Pro'. He was to become the chief suspect in Hoffa's disappearance.

Hoffa was playing a dangerous game – and one that was

of no benefit to his members. In effect, he was Mafia-izing the Union, handing it over to mobsters. The battle between American Labour and American Capital was turning into a battle between law and lawlessness. As Tony Pro increased his salary from $20,000 to $95,000 and brought in members of his family as Union stewards, the dues of the truckers vanished into the pockets of the gangsters. It was Boss Tweed all over again, but ten times as violent.

But law and order were putting up strong resistance. In 1951, Senator Estes Kefauver set up a Special Committee to Investigate Organized Crime. Kefauver had his attention drawn to Detroit, where one of the Teamsters' Locals was engaged in extortion and the 'protection racket'. In 1953, a committee heard that Hoffa had authorized Detroit Locals to destroy their financial records every year 'to save storage space'. The Committee began to focus its attention on Hoffa. And in 1956 an ambitious young man named Robert Kennedy also began to investigate the irregularities of the Teamsters' Union. He discovered that a gangster called Johnny Dio was running some of the Union Locals in New York. Following this trail, Kennedy discovered that Dave Beck, the president of the Teamsters, had embezzled over $350,000 from the Union. Investigators came to talk to Jimmy Hoffa. Kennedy invaded Hoffa's office, demanding to see the files. Hoffa threw him out. Kennedy returned with a subpoena, and Hoffa was forced to hand them over. Then, just as it began to look as if Hoffa and his Teamsters were in trouble, the investigation was called off. 'The pressure comes from way up there,' one committee member told reporters. It seems possible that this high-level intervention was due to the fact that the Teamsters had decided to support Michigan's Republicans in the 1954 elections.

From then on, Bobby Kennedy regarded Hoffa as his major quarry, and Hoffa regarded Bobby Kennedy as his worst enemy.

Murders

Senator Robert Kennedy, Hoffa's worst enemy

The first round went to Hoffa. A lawyer called John Cheasty, who was with the Internal Revenue Service, told Kennedy that Hoffa had attempted to bribe him. If proved guilty, Hoffa could have faced thirteen years in jail. The jury consisted of eight blacks and four whites. Copies of a black newspaper praising Hoffa as a friend of the working classes and showing a black attorney on his defence team were delivered at the homes of black jurors. Before the trial, the famous heavyweight, Joe Louis, appeared in court and put his arm around Jimmy Hoffa. To Kennedy's fury, Hoffa was found Not Guilty. Kennedy had gone on record as saying that he would jump off the Capitol if Hoffa wasn't convicted. Hoffa sent him a parachute with a note that said 'Jump'. Next, Hoffa appeared in court on a lesser charge of putting a wire tap on some of his own employees. The case ended in a mistrial.

In 1957, Dave Beck stepped down as president of the Teamsters and Hoffa was elected in his place.

Kennedy continued to try to draw the net around Hoffa, and Hoffa was contemptuous. He was certain that he was too powerful. His own members loved him, and as long as that was true, he felt he had nothing to worry about. He proved to be mistaken when a Grand Jury in Nashville, Tennessee charged him with extorting more than a million dollars from a haulage company. The case, in 1962, ended in a deadlocked jury, but when there were rumours that Hoffa had bribed jurors, the judge ordered an investigation. By now, Bobby Kennedy's brother John was President of the United States, and Hoffa was beginning to feel the pressure.

In the following year the Nashville Grand Jury indicted him for jury tampering, and a Grand Jury in Chicago for being involved in illegal loans amounting to $20,000,000 to various close acquaintances.

When John F. Kennedy was assassinated in November 1963, Hoffa hoped that he was seeing the light at the end of

President John F. Kennedy

the tunnel. But his trial in January 1964 proved him wrong. An ex-associate named Edward Grady Partin had decided to testify against a man he felt had seized too much power. He told how Hoffa sent him to bribe jurors, authorizing sums of $15,000 to $20,000. He also revealed, in a private discussion with the judge and lawyers, that Hoffa had discussed assassinating Robert Kennedy.

The defence tried to discredit Partin by dragging up his criminal past, but the jury was unconvinced. They found Hoffa guilty on two counts of jury tampering, and he was sentenced to eight years in prison and a $10,000 fine. There were several years of appeals, but on 7 March 1967 Hoffa began his sentence in the Lewisburg Federal Penitentiary.

Now, Hoffa made the biggest mistake of his life. He was determined to run the Teamsters' Union from prison, and he used Chucky O'Brien, the boy who had been brought up in Hoffa's family, as his contact man. The problem was to find someone to 'keep his chair warm', and who would not try to usurp his position. The man he chose was an old Hoffa loyalist named Frank Fitzsimmons, who had known Hoffa for thirty years, and who, during that time, had shown a dog-like devotion. Hoffa appointed Fitzsimmons general vice-president, a post he created especially for the occasion.

Also imprisoned with Hoffa was Tony Provenzano, serving four years for extortion. In spite of his incarceration, Tony Pro was still head of his New Jersey Local. There had been a time when he and Hoffa had been close allies, even friends. But now, for some reason, they seem to have taken a dislike to one another. It was said that Hoffa had asked Tony Pro to resign his position in the Teamsters' Union to avoid further embarrassment, and Tony Pro had sharply refused.

Even in prison, Hoffa could not help making use of his talent for organization. For the first time in his life he began

39

to read. He formed a grievance committee to carry the prisoners' complaints to the governor. He often found jobs for the Teamsters for prisoners who had served their time. The only good deed he probably came to regret was helping to get Tony Provenzano into hospital when he was suffering from some acute stomach complaint that would probably have killed him – Hoffa's loud protests led the authorities to change their mind and allow Tony Pro to go to an outside hospital.

The gangster showed himself less forgiving than Hoffa. Subsequently, there was a violent disagreement in the dining hall that ended by them being separated by other prisoners, while Provenzano shouted: 'Yours is coming!' After this, they ceased to speak to one another. When some of Hoffa's old friends in the Detroit mob sided with Tony Pro, he began to realize that he was being undermined.

Worse treachery was to come. The 'temporary' president of the Union, Frank Fitzsimmons, found that he was enjoying power – a private jet, a vast salary, a limitless expense account. Hoffa realized just how far the rot had set in when he sent Fitzsimmons a recommendation – virtually an order – about the new treasurer-secretary of the Union. Fitzsimmons ignored it, and gave it to his own man, another gangster.

In 1971, the parole board denied Hoffa's request for release, even though his wife Josephine had just suffered a heart attack. Hoffa's response was to decide not to stand at the next convention for re-election. He resigned all his offices with the Teamsters. At the convention, Hoffa was voted a lump-sum retirement pension of $1.7 million, but Fitzsimmons was given the job of president. A number of mobsters, including Tony Pro's brother, filled other positions with their own men. As a result, one mobster who had already borrowed $43,000,000 from Hoffa was able to borrow a further $27,000,000. Under Fitzsimmons, the

Union slipped into the hands of the Mafia, and they fought like sharks over its billion dollar pension fund.

At this point, Hoffa gained a surprising ally – President Richard Nixon. In the past, Hoffa and the Teamsters had been Nixon's faithful backers. Now, in exchange for similar support from Fitzsimmons for the next presidential campaign, Nixon agreed to pardon Hoffa – on condition that he refrained from all Union activity until 1980.

Hoffa later claimed that the version of the agreement he signed said nothing about refraining from Union activity – confining itself to a ban on carrying firearms, drug taking and excessive drinking.

When Jimmy Hoffa arrived back home in Michigan during Christmas 1971, and discovered what had happened, he was furious. The first thing was to get his old conviction for jury tampering overturned. The next was to get the ban on Union activity rescinded. For the next three years, Hoffa fought grimly to win his way back to power. Early in 1975 came what he considered the worst blow of all – his 'foster son' Chucky O'Brien went over to Fitzsimmons. He had quarrelled with Hoffa about his gambling debts.

Tony Pro was also showing his capacity for vindictiveness. He flatly turned down all Hoffa's peace overtures. He even sent Hoffa a message: 'I'm gonna snatch your granddaughter and put her eyes out.' Hoffa felt that he was perfectly capable of it. But he still refused when his supporters – and he still had many, particularly among the ordinary Teamsters – suggested a bodyguard. He said that it would make him careless. But in any case, he felt fairly certain that nobody would want to kill him.

What happened on 30 July 1975 seems to have proved him wrong. Some time after noon, he set out to some two o'clock meeting, without telling his wife where he was going, and left his summer home at Big Square Lake, forty miles outside Detroit and drove off in his Pontiac. At 2.30,

On 17 June 1934, the Brighton cloakroom attendants noticed an unpleasant smell in the office. The police traced it to a cheap-looking trunk, and it was opened in the police station. It was found to contain the torso of a woman wrapped in brown paper, and tied with window cord. A word written on the paper had been half obliterated by a bloodstain, but its second half read 'ford'. Cloakrooms all over the country were searched for the rest of the body, and the result was that a pair of legs was found in a suitcase at King's Cross.

The trunk and the suitcase had both been deposited on Derby Day, 6 June, between 6 and 7 in the evening; the person responsible had judged correctly that the cloakroom attendants would be too busy to remember customers. All the attendant could recollect was that the trunk had been left by a man.

Sir Bernard Spilsbury verified that the legs and trunk belonged to the same body, a woman in her mid-twenties who had been five months pregnant. The hairs on her legs were bleached with sunbathing and some light-brown hairs found on the body suggested a permanent wave – which indicated that she belonged to a reasonable income group. The brown paper in which the torso was wrapped had been soaked in olive oil – which might have suggested a restaurateur or some fairly well-to-do household. Yet although the crime was widely publicized, and over 700 missing women were traced, the identity of the victim remained a mystery. The maker of the trunk was found, in

Leyton, but he had no record of what shop it had
gone to. But one of his employees proved to have
written the word 'ford' on the paper. Five
thousand prenatal cases were traced and
eliminated. At last, the trunk was traced to a big
shop in Brighton, and it looked as if all this effort
was at last yielding some results, but once again,
clues simply ran out. The 'Brighton Trunk
Murderer' had proved that it was possible to
commit a perfect crime.

At the same time as the unsolved Brighton trunk
murder, another trunk murder in Brighton made
the police feel that they might have arrested the
culprit.

On 14 June 1934, a petty crook called Tony
Mancini was picked up by the police and
questioned about the Brighton trunk murder. He
was released, but fled to London. His landlady,
concerned about the smell coming from the trunk
he had left in his room in Kemp Street, Brighton,
opened it and saw that it contained a decaying
female corpse. Mancini was arrested while hitch-
hiking, and brought back to Brighton.

The dead woman proved to be forty-two-year-
old Violette Kaye, an ex-chorus girl who had
turned to prostitution. Mancini had moved in with
Violette, and had been supported by her. But she
was a woman of highly jealous disposition, and one
day started a furious argument in the café where
Mancini worked – the cause being a waitress with
whom Mancini was flirting.

Violette had died from a blow on the head, and

Sir Bernard Spilsbury was forced to admit in court that it could have been caused by a fall down the steps to the basement where she lived – particularly if she was drunk at the time. Mancini claimed that he had come home from work and found her lying dead, and then lost his nerve, knowing that he had a long police record.

Mancini was aquitted. But in 1976, forty-two years later, he confessed to a Sunday newspaper that he had, in fact, killed Violette Kaye in the course of a quarrel.

he telephoned his wife to ask if anyone had called. 'I've been stood up,' he snarled with disgust. That was the last she heard of her husband. When police found his Pontiac in the car park of the Machus Red Fox restaurant in Bloomfield, near Detroit, they half expected to find his body in the boot. It was empty. Tony Provenzano had a perfect alibi – he was in New Jersey, playing cards at the time Jimmy Hoffa disappeared. 'Jimmy was, or is, my friend,' he asserted without blushing.

Gangster Tony Giacalone, another suspect, also had an excellent alibi – he was in an Athletic Club at the time. Chucky O'Brien claimed that he had been in the same Athletic Club. When Hoffa's son James asked him to take a lie detector test, he refused. Sniffer dogs found Hoffa's scent in O'Brien's car, but that proved nothing.

Several months after Hoffa's disappearance, three mobsters from New Jersey, members of Tony Pro's Union, were named by witnesses, who claimed to have seen them in the car with Hoffa on the afternoon he disappeared. They were Savatori Briguglio, his younger brother Gabriel, and

Thomas Andretta. But when questioned by a Grand Jury, all three took refuge in the Fifth Amendment – the clause that allows a suspect not to answer questions that may incriminate him. A murderer-turned-informer named Ralph Picardo, serving a twenty-year sentence, told the jury that Andretta had come to see him in prison soon after Hoffa's disappearance, and Andretta's brother Stephen had told him that the Briguglio brothers had murdered Hoffa, placed his body in an oil drum and buried it in a rubbish tip.

Vincent Piersante, head of Michigan's Organized Crime Task Force, stated his own view that the disappearance of Jimmy Hoffa was due to an accident. His argument was that the mob would not dare to touch Hoffa because of the sheer scale of the investigation that would follow. In any case, Hoffa was a very long way from recovering his position in the Union. His theory was that Hoffa had died – perhaps of a heart attack – that afternoon in the course of a quarrel with the men he was meeting.

Another informer, Charles Crimaldi, told another story. He stated that Hoffa was involved with the Mafia in a plot to assassinate Fidel Castro, and that when he quarrelled with his associates, they decided to kill him to stop him from talking.

A more likely explanation lies in something that Hoffa confided to his son James during his prison years. He told him that, once he was back in control of the Union, he was going to undo the damage he had done, and boot the mob out of the Teamsters. Hoffa obviously believed he could do it. So, possibly, did the Mafia.

It seems a pity that it took Hoffa so long to reach a decision he should have made nearly forty years earlier.

Chapter Three

Who Killed
Georgina Moore?

In a book called *Murder By Persons Unknown*, by the crime writer H. L. Adam (1931) there is a chapter called 'Who killed Georgina Moore?'. The story he has to tell is this.

After lunch on 20 December 1881, a little girl named Georgina Anne Moore, aged seven and a half, went back to her school in Pimlico, and vanished. She was due home at about four o'clock. When she had failed to return by 4.30 her mother, Mrs Mary Moore, went out in search of her. Unable to find her, she sent a message to her husband Stephen, at the building site where he was working, telling him what had happened. Stephen Moore and several friends spent most of the evening and the rest of the night searching for Georgina, but there did not seem to be the slightest trace of her.

The next morning, Mary Moore was told by a little boy that he'd seen Georgina talking to a tall woman wearing a light Ulster some time after lunch the previous day. That sounded like their former landlady, Mrs Esther Pay, who wore this type of coat (an Ulster is a long overcoat made of frieze, a coarse woollen cloth).

In fact, Mary Moore had no reason to like Esther Pay. Esther's husband William had given the Moores notice when he discovered that Stephen Moore was having an affair with Esther. They had moved a short distance away, to Winchester Street. And Stephen had carried on his affair with Esther, sneaking into her bed in the early hours of the morning after her husband – whose job involved leaving the house very early – had gone to work. That summer, William Pay had found out that the affair was continuing, and he lost his temper with his wife and beat her up. After that, Stephen Moore had broken off the affair, telling Esther that it was for her own good. In fact, he had simply turned his amorous attentions elsewhere.

This is why Mary Moore went along to 51 Westmoreland Street to enquire whether Esther Pay had seen her daughter. Esther Pay evidently bore more of a grudge than Mary Moore did – she said coldly that she hadn't seen Georgie, and slammed the door.

The policeman who was placed in charge of the case, Inspector Henry Marshall of Scotland Yard, called on Esther on 5 January 1882, two weeks after the child's disappearance. Again she denied all knowledge of it. When she asked him why he had come to see her, he told her: 'Because there are rumours that you've taken the child away.' Esther insisted that she had an alibi – she had spent that afternoon with her sister-in-law, Carrie Rutter.

On 30 January 1882, a barge was travelling along the river Medway at Yalding, Kent, when the bargee, Alfred Pinhorn, found his hook was caught in something at the bottom of the river. He pulled and a child's body bobbed to the surface.

Lifted onto the tow-path, the body was seen to be tied with wire, with the legs fixed under the chin. It had been held down in the river by a large fire brick. It was covered in clay, and greatly decomposed.

Inspector Marshall was informed, and hurried down to Yalding. He had no doubt that he had found the body of Georgie Moore, particuarly when he learned that a child's white straw hat, trimmed with black velvet – of the kind Georgie was wearing when she vanished – had been found hanging on a bough over the river two weeks earlier. The inspector looked startled when he learned the name of the man who had found it; it was James Humphreys, and Esther Pay's unmarried name was Humphreys. James Humphreys was her uncle, and only two fields away, in the village of Nettlestead, Esther's parents lived in a cottage. In fact, Esther was there, staying with them, at the time the body was discovered.

This looked too much like coincidence.

Early the next morning, Stephen Moore arrived in Yalding and identified his daughter. Inspector Marshall then went to call on Esther Pay. She seemed indignant at the intrusion.

'How did you know I was here?'

'Have you not heard that yesterday a child was found in the Medway, at the back of your house?'

'No.'

'I must detain you,' said Marshall, 'on a charge of stealing the child. You may be charged with her death.'

Esther Pay's reply was: 'You must prove it.'

The police searched the house, and in a small handbag, they found a letter written by Esther to Stephen Moore. She called him 'darling', and asked him to write to her. 'If you hear any tidings,' said the letter, 'let me know at once. Poor little darling! I hope you will find her.'

Esther was taken to the local station, where she was left in charge of a police sergeant. To him she remarked: 'It's very strange to me if Moore doesn't know something about it. He's so artful. You'd better look after him, for I shouldn't be surprised if he's not missing very shortly; I know he's not on very good terms with his wife, and now he's got rid of Georgie you'd better look very sharp after him, for once he gets away you'll never catch him.'

She expressed the same kind of suspicion to Inspector Marshall when he came back. Stephen Moore was standing outside on the station platform, and Marshall had refused to let her speak to him. 'Don't be surprised if he bolts,' said Esther, 'and then you'll find the most guilty party is gone.' But later on the train, she seemed to contradict this statement, saying that she thought Georgina had been murdered to spite Stephen Moore. 'He has served women very badly, some that I know worse than me, and he has served *me* bad enough. Why don't you discover *them*, then you might get on the right track.'

In fact, Stephen Moore, a rather good-looking young man with a neatly trimmed handlebar moustache, was something of a Casanova. He had married his wife eight years earlier, after she had given birth to a son. They moved to Bath, where Georgina was born, and Moore began an affair with a lady called Emma Irwin, a widow who kept a grocer's shop, claiming that he was unmarried. She bore him a son, but the child lived for only three days. His wife seems to have found out about this, and went back to her parents, taking the two children with her. Moore moved to London, but continued his affair with Emma Irwin, but when he met her sister, Alice Day, decided that he would like to add her to his collection of mistresses. Like her sister, she succumbed. Not long after this, Mary Moore and the children came to rejoin him in London, and they took rooms at 51 Westmoreland Street, Pimlico. In 1879, Alice Day arrived declaring that she was pregnant. Moore denied all responsibility, and sent her away, never to see her again. When Emma Irwin learned what had happened, she also broke off with Stephen Moore.

But by now, Stephen Moore already had his eye on another potential mistress – Esther Pay. His landlord and landlady, the Rutters, had moved out of 51 Westmoreland Street, and Carrie Rutter's brother, William Pay, had moved in with his wife Esther. Esther was a tall, dark-haired woman of thirty-five, with a prominent nose and receding chin. Her firm mouth suggested a certain determination of character.

Murders

After William Pay had blacked his wife's eye, and Stephen Moore had decided that the affair was more trouble than it was worth, he broke with Esther 'for her own good' and promptly began affairs with two other women, a servant girl called Miss Carroll, and a Mrs Maidment, who lived near Regent's Park.

Three days after Georgina's disappearance, Esther called at the building company where Stephen Moore was working. He had now shaved off his moustache and whiskers, and Esther was apparently pleasantly impressed by his appearance. She told him she had come to talk to him about the missing child.

A few days before Georgina's body was discovered, they met again in Sloane Square, walked across Hyde Park, and stopped at a pub. He then went back to her lodgings – she had left her husband – and it seems that some kind of reconciliation took place. (This can be assumed from the affectionate tone of her letter to him.) She told him that she intended to go down to see her parents at Yalding the next day. We can also assume that the two had become lovers again from the fact that Moore met her again the next day at Charing Cross Station, and they walked down the Strand and had a glass of wine together after which he bought her some flowers and took her to the station.

On the evening that Esther was escorted back to London, she faced Stephen Moore from the dock in Westminster Police Court. Without meeting her eyes, Moore said: 'All along I have considered you innocent in this matter, but now that the body has been found so near your home I am of a different opinion. I think you must be implicated.' 'How can you say so?' Esther replied. 'Mind this isn't the means of your own character being investigated – which may bring out something you may not like.'

After this exchange, Esther was charged with the murder of Georgina Moore.

She was right about one thing. As the story of Stephen Moore's complicated love life became public property, he found himself violently unpopular. At Georgina's funeral, on 4 February, he was booed and hissed by the mob, and a cordon of policemen had to protect him from being attacked.

Esther Pay's trial opened at Lewis Assizes on 25 April 1882, and lasted for three days. The judge was Baron Pollock, the prosecution was led by Mr Henry Poland, and Esther Pay was defended by Mr Edward Clarke.

Poland's opening speech described how the Moores and the Pays had become acquainted when they lived in the same house, how Esther had apparently become fond of Georgina, and how Stephen Moore and Esther drifted into 'terms of improper intimacy'. He went on to tell how Moore had left his wife soon after he broke with Esther, and had moved in with Mrs Maidment near Regent's Park, staying with her about six months. In fact, he was still with Mrs Maidment when Georgina disappeared. He was evidently fond of his daughter, because he had insisted that she should go and spend Christmas with himself and Mrs Maidment. But a week before his daughter's body was found, Moore moved out of Mrs Maidment's house and moved back in with his wife.

Obviously, Stephen Moore was what would now be described as a bastard, and many women must have had a motive for revenge.

Poland went on to say that on the day of Georgina's disappearance, Esther Pay was not seen in London after 12.45, and she had still not returned to her house by eleven o'clock that night. What had happened in the meantime, according to Poland, was that Esther had picked up Georgina on her way to school, taken her down to Yalding, and there strangled her, bound her up with wire, and thrown her body in the river. A man in a nearby house had heard a child scream late at night.

51

If he was correct, then Esther must have taken the fire-brick and the length of wire with her in a bag when she went out to meet Georgina – which suggested that she must be singularly cold-blooded.

There was a stir of interest when Stephen Moore appeared in court. He admitted that he had been 'immorally connected' with Esther Pay, and had continued the affair with her even after her husband had thrown them out of the house. Of Esther he remarked: 'She was very kind to my daughter, and my daughter appeared to be very fond of her.'

Moore went on to admit that he'd left his wife in October to go and live with Mrs Maidment in Regent's Park. He told the story of his daughter's disappearance, of how he had subsequently met Esther, but tactfully left out the fact that he had been to her room.

In the course of his evidence, Moore admitted that, during his affair with Esther, he had been to visit her parents at Yalding. The admission lent support to those who believed that a man as wicked as Stephen Moore might well have had some motive for getting rid of his own daughter. Yet Moore's story made it clear that he had an unshakeable alibi – he had been at work at the time his daughter vanished.

At one point in the proceedings, it became apparent that Moore was even more immoral than anyone supposed. Asked if he had ever been through the marriage ceremony more than once, he replied that he could not answer the question for fear of incriminating himself. The Prosecution seems to have had some evidence that he was a bigamist.

He went on to admit that, working as a carpenter at a house in Kensington, he had met a young maidservant called Miss Carroll, and started an affair with her.

Asked about Mrs Maidment, he said that she had now returned to her husband.

The unsolved murder of five-year-old Willie Starchfield bears some resemblance to the case of Georgina Moore.

On 8 January 1914, a fifteen-year-old errand boy entered a compartment of the North London Railway train at Mildmay Park at about four in the afternoon. He noticed a small hand sticking out from beneath the seat, but was too frightened to examine it. At Dalston he tried to attract the attention of a porter, but failed. At the next station, Haggerston, he fled from the train, but then went and told the stationmaster. The train was halted at the next station, and the body of the five-year-old boy was found under the seat.

Willie Starchfield's mother and father were separated. His father, John Starchfield, sold newspapers in Tottenham Court Road. The boy lived with his mother Agnes in Hampstead Road. That day, he'd been sent on an errand at 12.50, but failed to return.

Doctor Bernard Spilsbury calculated that death had taken place some time between two and three o'clock. The body had then been pushed under the seat, and apparently the train had gone back and forth several times between Chalk Farm Station and Broad Street.

The next day, a search of the railway line uncovered a piece of cord not far from Shoreditch Station. It looked as if it had been dropped from a window of a passing train, and seemed to fit the groove around Willie Starchfield's throat.

Suspicion began to fall on the father, John

Starchfield. A Mrs Wood said that she was in
Kentish Town around one o'clock when she saw a
man leading a little boy by the hand. The boy was
eating a piece of currant cake and she remembered
his golden curls. A commercial traveller named
White saw the same little boy with the man at
Camden Town Station around two o'clock.

At the inquest, both the witnesses picked out
John Starchfield as the man they had seen.
Starchfield was arrested and charged with
murder.

The problem was, why should Starchfield want
to kill his own son? It seemed unlikely that he
would do this simply to spite his wife. Chief
Inspector William Gough theorized that Starchfield
had intended to try to persuade the boy to leave
his mother to live with him, had met him in the
street, and then persuaded him to go for a train
ride. On the train, Starchfield had probably tried to
persuade his son to leave his mother and come and
live with him. If Willie refused, despite all his
father's arguments, Starchfield may have lost his
temper and hit the boy. Then, perhaps in a fit of
rage, or to stifle his cries, he pulled a piece of cord
out of his pocket – the cord used to tie up bundles
of newspapers – and strangled him. Spilsbury said
that the child was in a condition of *status
lymphaticus*, which meant that he might easily die if
he received a severe shock.

Still another witness who knew Starchfield well
said that he saw Starchfield leading Willie by the
hand around two o'clock that day.

It looked an open and shut case, but when it
came into court on 9 March 1914, Gough realized
that his evidence was less strong than he had
hoped. A witness who knew Starchfield tried to
commit suicide before he could appear in court.
Mrs Wood admitted that she had seen Starchfield's
photograph in a newspaper before she identified
him, and was confused about the kind of hat he
was wearing when she saw him. The judge
criticized the coroner for inefficiency, and told the
jury to return a verdict of Not Guilty.

Starchfield died two years later, still strongly
protesting his innocence, and insisting that the
crime had been committed by somebody as an act
of revenge. In 1912 he had helped arrest an armed
madman who had been firing at random in the bar
of a hotel. Starchfield was wounded in the struggle,
and awarded one pound a week by the Carnegie
Heroes' Fund. Starchfield thought that it was some
friend of the madman, Stephen Titus, who had
murdered his son. Chief Inspector Gough remained
convinced that Starchfield was the killer.

He was finally asked if he knew the whereabouts of
various ex-mistresses on the day his daughter disappeared.
He had to admit that he had no idea of where Mrs Irwin or
Alice Day had been at the time, but he was fairly certain
that Mrs Maidment and Miss Carroll were nowhere near
Pimlico when his daughter disappeared.

The main thrust of the prosecution was clear. Georgina
Moore had been murdered by one of Stephen Moore's
ex-mistresses; the motive was revenge, and all the circum-

stantial evidence pointed to Esther Pay as being the killer.

The prosecution now began to accumulate circumstantial evidence. The ill-used Mrs Moore, obviously in a state close to collapse, told how Esther Pay had been very kind to Georgina and used to take her out and buy her sweets and toys. Georgina, she said, was a very timid child. The implication was clear. Georgina would not have gone with a stranger, but she *would* have gone with Esther Pay.

A little boy of seven testified that he had seen Georgina with Esther Pay after lunch on the day that she had disappeared. The child, whose name was Arthur Harrington, had been taken to an identity parade to see whether he could recognize the woman he had seen with Georgina, and immediately went and touched Esther Pay.

A policeman named Hill then testified how, shortly after two o'clock on the day Georgina disappeared, he had seen a woman and child walking towards Ebury Bridge. He said that the woman was wearing a light Ulster and that she wore a black hat. Later, he also identified Esther Pay in an identity parade.

Yalding could not be reached directly from Charing Cross, and passengers had to change trains at Paddock Wood. After PC Hill, a man called Charles Barton, who ran a kind of horse-cab (fly) service from Paddock Wood, told how one day around Christmas, he had been approached by a woman and child, soon after 4.12 in the afternoon (the London train arrived in Paddock Wood at 4.12). He had not been able to tell whether the child was a boy or a girl, because he was very short-sighted. The woman wanted to know the cab fare to Yalding, and when he said four shillings, she looked disappointed and said: 'So much?' He told her that she could get there for three pence on the train, and that there was a train due in a few minutes. She made the curious reply: 'I don't want to go by train.' He said that it had struck him as odd that a woman should enquire about a cab to Yalding when she could so easily take the train for a fraction of the cost.

The next witness was a nineteen-year-old youth who had known Esther Pay in the earlier days when she was Esther Humphreys. He described how, about a week before Christmas, he was standing in front of the Kent Arms at about quarter past four in the afternoon when he saw a woman and a little girl go by, and that the woman was wearing an Ulster and carrying a bag or parcel. The child was walking behind her, evidently tired, and the woman said: 'Come along, my dear.' As she passed him he recognized her as Esther Humphreys. Oddly enough, when taken to an identity parade, he had failed to pick out Esther Pay, although she had recognized him. This was the first point that was clearly in Esther's favour.

Three more witnesses claimed to have seen a woman and child on the same afternoon. One of them was the wife of a pub landlord in Brenchley, which is south of Paddock Wood (Yalding is to the north-east). She told how, on the afternoon of 20 December, between four and five o'clock, a strange woman came in and had a large gin just inside the door. (The actual measure was a half quartem, an eighth of a pint.) She was carrying a parcel. She admitted that she had not seen a child with the woman, and asked whether she recognized Esther in the dock replied that she did not. But a labourer called Stephen Barton, who followed her, said that he had been in the pub when the woman came in for gin, and when the woman left, he had looked out of the window and noticed that she had a child with her. The woman had been wearing a black veil, which may explain why the landlady failed to recognize her.

Thomas Judd, landlord of the New Inn, not far from Yalding, stated that on the night of 20 December, at about half past six, a woman and child went into the front room of the pub, and that he thought the child seemed very weary. The woman bought two pennyworth of biscuits, and gave the child one of them. She also had three penny-worth of whisky. Shown a photograph of Georgina Moore, he said that he thought it was the same child. They stayed about half an hour then went off. He heard the woman say to the child: 'Come, dear, eat your cake.'

A witness named George Bradley, a labourer who lived near the Railway Inn at Yalding, not far from where the child's body had been found, told of hearing a cry during the course of the evening from the direction of the river. He was not sure of the time, but thought it was somewhere towards nine o'clock – it might even have been later. He'd gone to the door to look out into the darkness, but could see nothing.

Various witnesses appeared who claimed that, the following morning, they had seen Esther Pay on Yalding station with her mother, Mrs Humphreys. (Later, Esther's father would insist Esther had not been home since the previous August, and that his wife could not have gone to the station with Esther on the morning of the 21st because she had such bad neuralgia that she had to wear a hand-kerchief around her head for more than a week.)

After this, the prosecution called various witnesses to try to blacken Esther Pay's character. One of them, a neigh-bour, told how Esther had told her that Stephen Moore was a very bad man, and that she would 'stick him' or 'shoot him.' Carrie Rutter, Esther Pay's sister-in-law – whom Esther had used as an alibi for the afternoon Georgina disappeared – now declared that it was not true that she and Esther had been shopping in Fulham Road on that afternoon. She'd not even seen Esther on 20 December. It was not until the 23rd that Esther had told her that she had had a 'spree' with a lady called Mrs Harris, but as she did not wish to get Mrs Harris into trouble, she wanted Carrie Rutter to claim that she and Esther had been out together that afternoon. It looks as if Esther had deliberately tried to create a false alibi.

The next day, the man who had analysed the contents of the dead child's stomach said that it looked like the kind of starch that was found in biscuits. The stomach contents also smelt of pineapple, which suggested that the child had eaten pineapple-favoured sweets not long before her death.

Soon after this, another witness testified that William Pay, Esther Pay's husband – and another obvious suspect – had been at work throughout the whole day of Georgina's disappearance.

That concluded the prosecution's case – and it was obviously a very strong one. It looked as if Esther had intercepted Georgina on her way to school that day, and told her some story – possibly that she had her mother's permission to take her down to Yalding. A train left Charing Cross at 2.52, and arrived at Paddock Wood at 4.12. Another train left Paddock Wood for Maidstone at 4.29, and would have reached Yalding a few minutes later. Yet, for some reason, the woman had preferred to take the child on a circuitous route by road rather than catching a train. Did not that suggest that she was anxious not to be seen getting off the train at Yalding with the child? Instead, she forced the tired seven-year-old to walk for miles, taking more than two hours. In Yalding, according to the prosecution, she had taken Georgina to the river bank, strangled her, and then thrown her body into the river, which was swollen with flood water. She tied her up with the wire that she probably carried in the parcel, and weighted her down with a brick which she had also brought with her from London. Then she went to the home of her parents, spent the night, and travelled back the following morning to London. She called on her sister-in-law two days later to arrange an alibi. And when questioned by Inspector Marshall, she claimed that she had spent the afternoon of Georgina's disappearance shopping with Carrie Rutter. She had told another friend that she had wanted to 'stick' or 'shoot' Stephen Moore. What could be more clear than that she had murdered the child out of a desire for revenge?

Edward Clarke (later Sir Edward) laboured mightily in her defence. Esther's seventy-two-year-old father, a bailiff who worked for a local hop farmer, testified that his daughter had definitely not returned home on the evening of 20 December. He was followed by Esther's mother, Mary Humphreys, who confirmed that she had not seen her daughter since the previous August Bank Holiday. She explained that she was suffering from such bad neuralgia between 15 December and 20 December that she had to wear a handkerchief around her face and was unable to go out. So she could not have been the woman who was seen on Yalding station with Esther the next morning.

Various other witnesses also gave evidence that Mrs Humphreys had been unwell during Christmas week.

Clarke then launched into his main speech for the defence. Surely, he said, no woman could possibly be barbarous enough to lure a child into the country, commit a horrible murder, and then fling her into the river. (He also suggested that it would take 'superhuman strength' to fling a body eight feet out into the stream.)

The alternative, he suggested, was that Georgina had been murdered in *London*, not long after she was last seen by her mother, and that her body was then taken down to Yalding and flung into the river there in an attempt to incriminate Esther. The wire had been tied so firmly that he believed that it must have been tied by a man. Moreover, whoever did it had left eight feet of wire between the body and the brick. If that person had meant the body to stay at the bottom of the river, he – or she – would surely have tied the brick to the body. Leaving eight feet of wire meant that the body would undoubtedly rise to the surface, and in due course be found – incriminating Esther.

If Esther had really abducted the child and taken her from Paddock Wood to Yalding by road, surely she would have avoided calling in crowded pubs, where she would be seen by several witnesses? In fact, most of the witnesses who claimed to have seen her that day had failed to identify her later.

Surely, he said, the fact that an undigested meal was found in the child's stomach suggested that the murder had not been committed at Yalding. All the child had eaten between Paddock Wood and Yalding – according to the landlord of the New Inn – was one biscuit.

Moreover, he said, no woman would have killed a child beside a river that was in flood – according to one witness, covering the towpath – and then waded through the water on the towpath to hurl the child and the brick more than eight feet into the water.

Even if Esther *had* taken the child all the way to Yalding to murder her, surely the last thing she would then have done would be to stay the night with her parents, and travel back from the local station the next morning, where she was almost sure to be seen and recognized?

When Clarke sat down, there was a brief rattle of applause which the judge quickly suppressed. There could be no doubt that Clarke had made the case against Esther seem rather absurd, and that many people in the court agreed with him.

All that now remained was for Mr Poland to make the final statement for the prosecution. He simply repeated his basic case – that Esther had not been seen in London since the afternoon Georgina Moore disappeared, until the following afternoon. In other words, she had been absent for twenty-four hours.

It was true, he admitted, that the evidence against Esther Pay was entirely circumstantial. But surely that circumstantial evidence was extremely convincing?

Murders

Judge Baron Pollock's summing-up was strictly fair and balanced. The jury had to make up its own mind what they could accept and what they could reject. If there was any doubt, the benefit of the doubt must be given to the prisoner.

On the other hand, he said, a woman and child had been seen at many stages travelling from London to Yalding via Paddock Wood, and he thought the evidence of the landlord of the New Inn was particularly convincing.

He dismissed the idea that Stephen Moore could have somehow murdered his own child. The fact that he was a dissolute and immoral man did not prove that he would take the life of his daughter. (No one had suggested that Stephen Moore had murdered his own child, and Pollock probably raised this possibility simply for the pleasure of calling Stephen Moore dissolute and immoral.)

At half past five on 28 April 1882, the jury retired. They were back twenty minutes later. The prisoner was brought up from her cell, and showed no sign of tension as the names of the jury were called out. Then the foreman of the jury announced that they found the prisoner Not Guilty. This time, the judge made no attempt to halt the applause, and Esther bowed to the jury and thanked them. With relatives embracing her, she was led from the courtroom.

H. L. Adam concludes his account of the trial: 'Mr Clarke made a splendid fight for the defence, and had the satisfaction of seeing his client acquitted.'

He goes on to ask whether there exists a more glaring instance of the fallibility of the British system of procuring evidence of identification than was to be found in the case of Esther Pay. 'Never, it is safe to say, were such feeble efforts employed to fix the identity of an accused person.'

The first witness who claimed to have seen her at Paddock Wood was the owner of the cab service, Charles Barton. He admitted to being short-sighted. But he also claimed that Esther said she did not know it was so far from

Paddock Wood to Yalding. That was absurd. As a native of the area, Esther would have known precisely how far it was from Paddock Wood to Yalding.

Adam goes on to talk about the number of people who claimed they had seen Esther on that road between Paddock Wood and Yalding, and mentions another famous case of mistaken identity, Adolf Beck, a man who was wrongly imprisoned for swindling, after a number of witnesses had identified him as the swindler. Later, the true culprit was found.

It is quite possible, Adam says, even probable, that all these people saw a woman, but they did not see Esther Pay. You could not conscientiously hang the proverbial dog on such evidence. The unsupported evidence of the labourer who said he heard a scream in the vicinity of the river is of very little significance. The evidence of the two women who thought they had seen Esther on Yalding station the next morning was disproved by Esther's parents.

Why, asks Adam, did Esther try to fake an alibi for the afternoon of Georgina's disappearance? 'The answer to that question is that on that day she had a secret meeting with another man, and she told the apocryphal story to cover that escapade, in case it should come to the knowledge of her husband.'

According to Adam, the hat found on the branch of the tree was highly significant. It had probably caught there when the body was thrown into the river – which indicates that the water must have been very high indeed that night. It was far too high for a woman to have stood upon the bank and strangled a child.

Like Edward Clarke, Adam then points out that 'the wire round the body was thick and very firmly wound, suggesting the strength and skill of a man's hand'. Whoever threw the body into the river at that point wanted to incriminate Esther.

Murders

Adam concludes: 'As to who really did commit the murder, the reader must satisfy himself. It appeared to have been no secret to either judge or counsel in the case. As has already been described, the child was a timid one, and would not go away with anybody strange to her. The motive was revenge. It was not Esther, for she was very fond of the child, and had even talked of adopting it. She had no quarrel with Moore.

'If the police had not been led astray by the preconceived idea of Esther Pay's guilt, and had been so absorbed in the task of procuring her conviction, they might well have taken the real culprit. Afterwards it was too late.'

What Adam means is perfectly clear – the real culprit was Esther's husband William, who had a motive of revenge against Stephen Moore. The child knew him as well as she knew his wife – she would certainly have gone with him.

In *Killers Unknown* (1960) the crime writer John Godwin echoes Adam's opinion. In a chapter called 'The Martyrdom of Esther Pay' he concludes that at least one other person had a motive for killing Georgina: 'The person, of course, was Mr Pay. He had vowed to "get even" with Stephen Moore, and he had often enough threatened his wife with the same fate. The killing of Georgina fulfilled both threats at one stroke – the "masher" lost his child and the faithless spouse – very nearly – her life.'

Unfortunately, John Godwin's account contains many errors and even inventions. Inspector Henry Marshall becomes Detective Inspector Moon, Esther is described as 'one of the prettiest girls in the district' when a glance at her picture reveals that she could never have been anything of the sort. His account of the trial is brief but inaccurate. But, like Adam – whose account of the case he has obviously used – Godwin agrees that the not guilty verdict 'was the logical result of the utter failure of the single-track line taken by the prosecution. The police had used all their

64

energies in trying to prove, somehow, that Esther had taken Georgina to the river at Yalding on 20 December. But even if the Crown witnesses had been less obviously fuddled, the journey – as described by them – still wouldn't have made sense.'

This is a curious assertion. Surely the main point of the prosecution evidence was to try to prove that Esther had been seen again and again from the moment she picked up Georgina Moore to about an hour before she reached Yalding? It hardly seems logical to say that by concentrating on this evidence, the prosecution somehow destroyed its own case. What other course was open to them?

For almost a century, these two accounts – by H. L. Adam and John Godwin – have been the only available descriptions of the case. Then, in 1987, Bernard Taylor discussed it in a long chapter of a book called *Perfect Murder*, on which Taylor and Stephen Knight collaborated. Here, for the first time, all the evidence is reviewed sensibly.

What Taylor makes very clear is that the talk about the 'martyrdom of Esther Pay' is sentimental nonsense. There can be no possible doubt that Esther Pay murdered Georgina Moore.

This is a matter of simple logic. The body of Georgina Moore was found within a few hundred yards of the house of Esther Pay's parents. This means that either Esther Pay murdered her, or that somebody set out to point the finger of guilt at Esther Pay. Who could that somebody have been? Not Stephen Moore – he had no reason to murder his own daughter, and in any case, had a perfect alibi. Not one of Moore's ex-mistresses – unless one of them was vengeful enough to want to inflict simultaneous misery on Moore and Esther.

According to Adam and Godwin, the killer was William Pay, Esther's husband. What both Adam and Godwin take care not to mention is that the prosecution case ended with several witnesses testifying to the fact that William Pay had been at work all day on the day Georgina disappeared. Like Stephen Moore, he was a working man. If he had been absent on the day of Georgina's disappearance, he would have been the prime suspect. But William Pay had an absolutely unshakeable alibi.

So it is quite impossible that William Pay can have murdered Georgina. In any case, all the witnesses agreed that it was a *woman* who was seen with the child travelling down to Yalding, not a man.

Adam's comparison with the case of Adolf Beck is highly misleading. Beck, who was arrested in 1896 when one of his victims thought she recognized him walking down Victoria Street, in fact bore a strong resemblance to the real swindler, Wilhelm Meyer, alias John Smith. Esther Pay did not bear the slightest resemblance to her husband William. Or is Adam suggesting that some other woman, who *did* resemble Esther, actually abducted the child and took her down to Yalding?

One major question remains – the motive. One argument of the defence is certainly correct – that it could not have been revenge. Why should Esther want to 'revenge' herself on Stephen Moore? He had not betrayed her – he had betrayed his wife. And Esther had betrayed her husband. When the husband found out, he threw the Moores out of his house. Even so, Stephen Moore continued to slip into Esther's house when her husband had gone to work. Finally, after William Pay had found out, and blacked his wife's eye, Moore decided that it was time to separate. Esther may have regarded the decision as cowardly, but she had no reason to feel betrayed. Moore had not left her for another woman – at least as far as she knew.

Then why did Esther do it? Even the perceptive Bernard Taylor fails to see the reason which is staring him in the face. Three days after Georgina's disappearance, Esther called on her ex-lover at his place of work, and flattered him about his appearance now he had shaved off his moustache and whiskers. They talked about the missing child. After that, he saw her in the company of Inspector Marshall, at her home. Then, on 27 January, they met in the evening *at her request*, walked across Hyde Park, stopped in a pub for a drink, then returned to the house in Lower Sloane Street where she had just taken lodgings. She had left her husband. The next day, they met at Charing Cross Station, walked down the Strand and had a glass of wine, after which he bought her some flowers and they had tea together before she caught the train down to Yalding. That weekend, she wrote him two letters, both beginning 'darling', and suggesting unmistakably that they were lovers again.

The conclusion is obvious. Georgina was fond of Esther, and Esther was apparently fond of Georgina. Moore knew this. So the death of Georgina would forge a bond between them. Esther's murder of Georgina Moore was a calculated attempt to lure back her lover, and if possible, to enter a long-term relationship. She very nearly succeeded.

So there *is* a sense in which Stephen Moore was as responsible for the death of his daughter as the woman who actually strangled her.

Chapter Four

The Maybrick Mystery

On 8 August 1889, Florence Maybrick was sentenced to death for the murder of her husband James Maybrick by arsenic poisoning. She was subsequently reprieved, and served fifteen years in prison.

Yet in a book called *Great Unsolved Mysteries*, published in the 1930s, there is a chapter by J. S. Fletcher called 'The Maybrick Poison Trial'. What is the Maybrick case doing in a volume of unsolved mysteries?

Let Mr Fletcher tell the story for himself.

'In the August of 1889, being on a walking tour in the north of England, I turned one evening into the market place of a very small country town to find a crowd of several hundred people massed before the front of a local newspaper office, in the window of which at that very moment a boy was pasting up a large sheet of paper on which certain words had been written in staring letters. Presently I read these words for myself. There were eight in number – MRS MAYBRICK FOUND GUILTY AND SENTENCED TO DEATH.

'Who was this woman in whose fortunes the folk of that obscure little town, a hundred miles away from the assize court in which she had stood her trial for murder, were showing such intense interest that August evening?

'Born Florence Elizabeth Chandler, the daughter of an American banker, she had married in 1881, at the age of eighteen, a Liverpool cotton broker, James Maybrick, who

Mrs James Maybrick

at the time of the marriage was a man of forty-one. With him she settled down at Aigburth, and in due course bore him two children.

'That the marriage was not a happy one may be gathered from the fact that in its ninth year Mrs Maybrick took to herself a lover, one (Alfred) Brierley, with whom in March 1889 she spent three nights at a London hotel.

'Returning from London, she went, next day, with her husband, to the Grand National Steeplechase. Brierley was encountered there; somehow an altercation arose; Maybrick, when he and his wife reached the house, assaulted her, giving her a black eye.

'She prepared to leave him at once; friends intervened, a peace was patched up; later she claimed that Maybrick had been made aware of, and had condoned, her adultery.

'Very soon after this – April 1889 – Maybrick became seriously ill.

'Now let us consider what manner of man James Maybrick was. It would appear that his wife had had reason for some time, probably during most of their married life, to complain of his relations with other women; it may be that his infidelities turned her to Brierley.

'But – in view of what followed – that is not such an important matter as another which was well known to Maybrick's circle of acquaintance. Maybrick was a drug addict. He was in the habit of perpetually dosing himself with certain drugs such as strychnine and arsenic, probably because he knew them to be aphrodisiac in their effect.

'His intimate friends knew this; his business acquaintances knew it. More evidence on this point might have been given at the trial than was given. I myself, visiting Liverpool after the trial, and making certain enquiries into the matter, was introduced to a chemist who told me that Maybrick was "in and out of the shop all day long" seeking a dose of one of his favourite pick-me-ups. And in those doses arsenic figured largely.

'Maybrick's illness assumed alarming aspects on 27 April; he himself attributed it to an overdose of strychnine. He grew rapidly worse; doctors and nurses were installed, Mrs Maybrick, naturally, did a certain amount of nursing.

'On 11 May Maybrick died. Two days later a post-mortem examination was made by three doctors, who decided that death was due to inflammation of the stomach set up by some irritant poison. Next day Mrs Maybrick was arrested, and on the same day the Coroner's inquest was opened and adjourned.

'It was resumed on 25 May and again on 6 June, when evidence of the discovery of arsenic in the dead man's body was given. The Coroner's jury then returned a verdict of wilful murder against Mrs Maybrick, who in the meantime had twice been before the magistrates – the first time in her own bedroom.

'On 14 June the magistrates committed her for trial, and on 31 July she was placed in the dock at Liverpool Assizes, before Mr Justice Stephen, and charged with the wilful murder of her husband. The prosecuting council for the Crown was Mr Addison, QC, Mrs Maybrick was defended by that great man Sir Charles Russell, afterwards Lord Russell of Killowen, Lord Chief Justice of England.

'What was the evidence against her? A few days before her husband was taken seriously ill, Mrs Maybrick called at a chemist shop in Aigburth, and making some remark about flies being troublesome just then bought a dozen fly-papers.

'Two or three days later she called at another chemist shop in the neighbourhood and bought a further two dozen fly-papers. All these fly-papers, of course, contained arsenic.

'On 24 April she was seen by two of her servants to soak

these papers in a basin of water in her bedroom. Her own explanation of this was that she wanted to get a solution of arsenic for use as a cosmetic. Some time previously, according to her plea, an American doctor had given her a prescription for a face-wash, and she had lost it; knowing that it contained arsenic, and having heard from a friend that arsenic could be procured from fly-papers, she had purchased a supply.

'There was a certain amount of evidence as to Mrs Maybrick's opportunities of introducing arsenic into her husband's medicine and food, and in particular into a bottle of meat juice. By 5 May certain members of the household began to suspect that something was wrong, and Maybrick's brother Michael (known to the musical world as Stephen Adams, composer of many popular songs of the time) was summoned from London.

'From the time of his arrival, whether she knew it or not, Mrs Maybrick was suspect; Michael Maybrick, indeed, lost no time in communicating his suspicion to the doctors.

'The evidence for the prosecution spread itself over the best part of four days. Summarized, it amounted to an attempt to prove that Maybrick died of arsenical poisoning, and that the arsenic had been administered to him by his wife.

'Sir Charles Russell, as counsel for the prisoner, did his best to bring rebutting evidence and to prove to the jury that – to use his own words they "had no safe resting-place on which they could securely and satisfactorily justify to themselves that this was a death due to arsenical poisoning".

'It may be that after hearing Sir Charles's speech, and the medical evidence which he called, and if the defence had been left at that, the jury, whatever the Judge's summing-up proved to be, would have been disposed to, and would have returned, a verdict of acquittal. But Sir Charles allowed his client to make a statement.

72

'Mrs Maybrick spoke, of course, from the dock – in those days prisoners were not allowed to give evidence. She said little in the way of explanation and protest.

'When she had finished, Sir Charles asked leave to call two witnesses to whom she had made the same statement before the inquest. Mr Justice Stephen refused the request – as indeed he was bound to. And after Sir Charles's closing speech, and Mr Addison's closing speech, and the Judge's summing-up, the jury having deliberated little more than half an hour, returned a verdict of guilty, and Mrs Maybrick, having once more protested her innocence, was sentenced to death.

'The public immediately turned against the verdict. A vast crowd, assembled outside the Assize Court, hooted and hissed Mr Justice Stephen as he passed to his carriage. The newspaper press expressed astonishment at the result of the trial. Petitions for the Home Office poured in from all parts of the country.

'Meetings of protest were held in London and Liverpool. Members of Parliament and men eminent in many professions joined in the widespread agitation so quickly aroused on Mrs Maybrick's behalf; the Queen herself was approached.

'Eventually, on what was practically the eve of the execution, the sentence was commuted to one of penal servitude for life. Mrs Maybrick served fifteen years imprisonment – at Woking and Aylesbury – and being released from the last-named prison in January 1904, left England for America.

'I will now venture to give my reasons for considering this to be the most unsatisfactory trial for murder ever held in an English Court of Justice.

'Let us begin with the man who presided over it, Sir James Fitzjames Stephen. He was a man of the greatest eminence in his time – a great writer and authority on criminal law, and as a judge scrupulously just and anxiously considerate to those who came before him. But was he in full possession of his great powers at the time of the great Maybrick trial?

'Four years previously, while holding the Assize at Derby – 1885 – he had suffered a stroke of paralysis, and had had to retire from all work for a time; two years after he sentenced Mrs Maybrick to death his mind gave way altogether. Was he fit for his work when he tried Mrs Maybrick?

'My old friend, the late H. B. Irving, as expert a criminologist as he was great as an actor, with whom I have discussed the Maybrick affair more than once, and who edited an account of the trial, has this to say about the summing up:

"It is anxious and painstaking, indeed, over anxious. At times, the Judge seems almost overweighted by the gravity and difficulties of the case. His grasp of the case is by no means sure, and there are errors in dates and facts and in the recapitulations of the evidence that would hardly have been expected in a Judge of Sir James Stephen's experience."

'Clearly, Sir James Stephen was not – mentally – in a condition to preside over a trial the issue of which was life or death for the unfortunate woman in the dock.

'But there was more than this. Unconsciously, no doubt, Sir James Stephen created an atmosphere of prejudice against Mrs Maybrick. In addressing the Grand Jury (and, of course, his remarks went forth through the Press *urbi et orbi* – to the city and the world), he laid undue, unjustifiable stress on Mrs Maybrick's relations with Brierley.

"I hardly know how to put it otherwise," said Mr Justice Stephen, "than this – that if a woman does carry on an adulterous intrigue with another man, it may supply every sort of motive – that of saving her own reputation; that of breaking through the connection, which, under such circumstances, one would think would be dreadfully painful to the party to it. It certainly may quite supply – I won't go further – *a very strong motive as to why she should wish to get* rid *of her husband."*

'Is there any wonder that millions of people, when the trial came to an end, said that Mrs Maybrick was being punished for her temporary infidelity, for her three nights of adultery, and not for murder? Is there any wonder, either, that when the Clerk of Arraigns asked Mrs Maybrick if she had anything to say why sentence of death should not be pronounced upon her, she answered: "I was guilty of intimacy with Mr Brierley, but I am not guilty of this crime."

'But there was another atmosphere of prejudice against this unfortunate woman. At the end of the first day's magisterial proceedings, she was loudly hissed as she left the court by a number of women who had contrived to secure admission.

'She herself so felt that it would be impossible to get a fair trial from a Liverpool jury that she besaught her legal advisors to get the venue of the trial removed to London.

'It was not until after long and anxious thought and consultation that her solicitors decided to face a trial in Liverpool, and, as a matter of fact, the jury empanelled in her case was not a Liverpool, but a Lancashire jury.

'That the jury did what it felt to be its duty, according to its lights, no one who knows anything of our English jury system will doubt, but their verdict did not satisfy a public which could read the evidence, and especially the medical evidence, for itself.

'For the medical evidence, to say the least of it, was contradictory. The Home Office expert of those days, Doctor Stevenson, said he had "no doubt that Maybrick had died from the effects of a poisonousness of arsenic".

'But Doctor Tidy, an equally great authority of that period, was just as positive in the other direction – he "completely negated the suggestion of death from arsenical poisoning".

'When the trial was over, Mr Auberon Herbert, in a letter to *The Times*, very pertinently asked whether it was necessary to inquire what irritant may have set up gastroenteritis in Maybrick, when his stomach had for some days been used as "a druggist waste-pipe", and was found to contain traces of strychnine, arsenic, jaborandi, cascara, henbane, morphia, prussic acid, papawi, iridin, and all the other medicines that had been administered in the course of his brief illness.

'And in a letter to the same newspaper Mr (afterwards Lord) Fletcher-Moulton probably hit the real truth when he said that Maybrick's death was "due to natural causes operating upon a system in which a long course of arsenic-taking had developed a predisposition to gastroenteritis".

'The Maybrick case was admirably summarized, three years after Mrs Maybrick had disappeared to Woking, in a petition carefully prepared by Lumleys, the solicitors, for presentation to Mr Asquith, the Home Secretary. I will further summarize it.

'1. There was no evidence that James Maybrick died from other than natural causes.

'2. There was no evidence that he died from arsenical poisoning.

'3. There was no evidence that his wife administered or attempted to administer arsenic to him.

'4. The verdict was against the weight of evidence.

'5. The jury did not give the prisoner the benefit of the doubt suggested by the disagreement of the expert (medical) witnesses.

'But the agitation kept up on Mrs Maybrick's behalf produced no effect on our Home Office.

'Sir Charles (by that time Lord) Russell did everything in his power to effect his client's release, but year after year went by and nothing was done.

'It is said that Lord Russell firmly believed in his client's innocence.

'Her trial was the most miserable muddle ever seen in an English court of law, and the only good thing that came out of it was that it helped, in some degree, to bring about the establishment of the Court of Criminal Appeal.'

The year after the trial, 1890, Mrs Maybrick's mother – the Baroness von Roques – discovered an interesting piece of evidence that suggested Florence's innocence. In Florence's bible, she found a slip of paper, in the hand of a certain Doctor Bay of New York, with a prescription for a face-wash to be applied with a sponge twice a day, and the ingredients included arsenic – just as Florence had claimed.

Florence was released from prison in 1904. She returned to America under the pseudonym Rose Ingraham, where she wrote a book called *Mrs Maybrick's Own Story: My Lost Fifteen Years*. For a time, she became a well-known lecturer, always insisting upon her innocence. In 1918, she moved to a town called Gaylordsville, Connecticut, where she purchased an acre of land for sixty dollars, and had a small house built for twelve hundred dollars. There she lived quietly for the rest of her life, often in considerable poverty – although many friends who believed in her innocence sent her small sums of money.

She returned twice to England, in 1911 and 1927. In 1911, she was shocked to hear of the death of her son James (known as Bobo) who had accidentally drunk a beaker of potassium cyanide to wash down a sandwich in April 1911. When she came to England again in 1927, she attended the Grand National, and gave an interview to the *Sunday News* in which she commented: 'It seems terrible that the children I risked my life to bring into the world should think their mother guilty of the crime that left them fatherless.' Either she had forgotten that Bobo was dead, or she had had more children. There seems to be a strong possibility that she was pregnant when she went into prison in 1889 – possibly by Brierley – and evidence has since indicated that she may have had an illegitimate child when she was only sixteen. She also said that she felt that she was on the point of death, and went to see her solicitors.

In fact, she lived on until October 1941, when she finally died at the age of seventy-nine.

And that, apparently, was the end of the Maybrick case . . . yet there was still a small but extremely strange footnote to be added to it.

One day in the spring of 1991, a Liverpudlian named Mike Barrett called on a friend named Tony Devereux, who was suffering from a fractured hip. Mike had recently been doing his shopping and helping him in other ways.

Tony Devereux handed Barrett a brown paper parcel. 'Take it. I want you to have it. Do something with it.'

Mike Barrett took it home, and discovered that the parcel contained what looked like a Victorian scrapbook, bound in black calf, and its first forty-eight pages had been cut out with a knife. The remainder contained what appeared to be some sort of a journal, written in a scrawl that was occasionally illegible. It began halfway through a sentence: '. . . what they have in store for them they would stop this instant.' The first half of the sentence was obviously 'if they knew'. He goes on: 'But do I desire that? my answer is no. They will suffer just as I. I will see to that. Received a letter from Michael perhaps I will visit him. Will have to come to some sort of decision regards the children. I long for peace of mind but I sincerely believe that that will not come until I have sought my revenge on the whore and the whore master.'

It goes on: 'Foolish bitch, I know for certain she has

arranged a rendezvous with him in Whitechapel. So be it, my mind is firmly made. I took refreshment at the Poste House it was there that I finally decided London it shall be. And why not, is it not an ideal location? Indeed do I not frequently visit the Capital and indeed do I not have legitimate reason for doing so. All who sell their dirty wares shall pay, of that I have no doubt. But shall I pay? I think not I am too clever for that.' He turned to the end of the diary and discovered that it was signed: 'Yours truly, Jack the Ripper.' It was dated: 'This third day of May 1889.'

It had been on that day that Maybrick was suddenly taken ill again after a Turkish bath. He had severe pains in the legs, and the doctor gave him a dose of morphine. He died eight days later at 8.30 in the evening.

A closer study of the diary convinced Mike Barrett that it had been written – or the author wanted it believed that it had been written – by James Maybrick. And the 'revenge on the whore' that Maybrick speaks of was the murder of prostitutes – the Jack the Ripper murders.

He rang a London publisher, who advised him to find himself a literary agent. As a result of this advice, he met Doreen Montgomery of Rupert Crew Ltd in London. On the day Mike Barrett called at her office with the diary, Doreen Montgomery invited one of her authors, Shirley Harrison, who was interested in the Maybrick case, to come along too.

The result of the meeting was that Shirley Harrison decided to write a book trying to prove that James Maybrick was Jack the Ripper.

Unfortunately, Mike Barrett had indiscreetly mentioned to a journalist he met on a train that he had found the diary. In April 1993, the *Liverpool Post* published the story about the diary, and the suspicion that Maybrick was Jack the Ripper. The publisher, Robert Smith of Smith Gryphon, was disgusted – he had been hoping to keep the diary a secret until its publication, and this premature disclosure would obviously reduce its impact.

What the diary appeared to show was that Maybrick was in a state of manic jealousy about his young wife Florence. About two years after their marriage (in 1881) she had discovered that her husband had a mistress and five children, two of whom had been born since their marriage. After the violent quarrel that followed, Florence moved into her own bedroom, and denied her husband his marital rights.

James's jealousy increased when he heard Florence tell his younger brother Edwin at a dinner party: 'If I had met you first things might have been different.' There seems to be a strong possibility that Florence and Edwin became lovers. Florence also carried on an affair with a London lawyer named Williams. Finally, early in 1888, she met a successful cotton broker named Alfred Brierley, a good-looking young bachelor, and started an affair with him. Whether Brierley is the 'whore master' referred to in the diary is a matter for speculation. At one point in the diary, Maybrick blames a man called Thomas Lowry for turning him into a murderer.

The diary makes it very clear that the author possesses a sadistic streak – that killing and disembowelling women, then running his hands through their entrails, produced a sense of savage power.

As rumours of the diary leaked into other newspapers, the general view was as the publisher had anticipated – distinctly sceptical. And in September 1993, it was announced that a New York handwriting expert, Kenneth Rendell, had analysed the ink in the diary, and declared that it dated from 1921 (give or take twelve years) and that therefore the diary had to be a forgery. As a result of this comment, the American publisher of the diary decided to pulp the whole edition. Yet Rendell's conclusion raised an obvious problem. If the diary was written as early as 1921 –

perhaps even as early as 1909 – then who had written it, and where had it been since then? If some hoaxer had decided to write the diary more than half a century before it was discovered, why had he not carried the hoax to its conclusion and made sure that the diary was found? Besides, it was the view of many 'ripperologists' who had seen the diary that it had to be a *modern* fake – written after 1986. If anything, Rendell's comments seemed to suggest that the diary was genuine – or was it not more likely that his ink-dating was twenty years out than that the diary was not written by an unknown hoaxer in the first part of the twentieth century?

When *The Diary of Jack the Ripper*, by Shirley Harrison, was published on 7 October 1993, the reaction of critics was negative. There seemed to be a vague and completely unjustified notion that it had been proved a fraud. In fact, at a conference of ripperologists a few months before publication, almost everyone there – with the exception of the present writer – had been convinced that the diary was a fake, and one expert had declared: 'As soon as the Diary is published, somebody is going to jump up and say, "I forged it and this is how I did it."'

In fact, no solid evidence to disprove the genuineness of the diary has appeared in the two years since its publication.

On the other hand – one interesting new piece of information *has* appeared. Paul Feldman, the producer of the video *The Diary of Jack the Ripper* set out with enormous persistence to try to trace the diary's provenance. At first, he was inclined to believe that it had been taken from Battlecrease House, the home of James and Florence Maybrick, which had since been turned into flats, and which had recently undergone some extensive repairs. Feldman believed that the diary might have been found under the floorboards by a workman. Then he learned that Mike Barrett's wife Anne had, at one point, actually worked in the office which had formerly been the site of Maybrick and Co. He now concentrated on the possibility that Maybrick might have left the diary somewhere in the office, and that Anne Barrett had eventually found it.

But when he learned that Anne Barrett's unmarried name had been Graham, this opened up a new line of enquiry. When she travelled to America after leaving prison, Florence Maybrick had called herself Mrs Ingraham, and the crime writer Nigel Morland states that Florence also used the name Graham. Was it conceivable that Anne Barrett – formerly Graham – was a direct descendant of James Maybrick?

As he pursued his enquiries, Paul Feldman one day received a phone call from Anne Barrett, whose sister had rung her to tell her that Paul Feldman had been questioning her. Anne Barrett now offered to tell Paul Feldman the true story of how her husband had come into possession of the diary. Mike Barrett, according to Anne, had been telling the truth. He had received the diary from Tony Devereux. But Anne claimed that she had given the diary to Tony Devereux.

Why? The diary had been in her family for many years – she saw it for the first time in 1968. It had been in an old tin trunk belonging to her father, Billy Graham. In due course, her father, about to remarry, passed on the diary to Anne. She disliked it – she felt there was something unpleasant about it – and jammed it behind a cupboard.

Her husband had started drinking heavily, and they were hardly on speaking terms. But Mike wanted to be a writer – he had even taken a course in writing. Anne thought that the diary might provide him with a starting point of a book. But she was anxious that he should not pester her father Billy. So she hit upon the device of approaching Tony Devereux, and asking if he would pass on the diary. So this, according to Anne Barrett, is how her husband came to be in possession of the diary.

There is evidence to suggest that Florence Maybrick had an illegitimate child in Liverpool when she was sixteen. Paul Feldman believes that this child was given the name Graham and was 'farmed out'. (Florence crossed between England and America many times between her childhood and teens, and is known to have been in Liverpool in 1878.)

Paul Feldman believes that the illegitimate child was William Graham, the father of Billy Graham, and that the diary was passed on to him in 1941, after the death of Florence Maybrick, by Florence's solicitors.

If Anne Barrett's story is true – and it seems difficult to suggest a reason why she should have invented it – then the diary *was* known to Florence, and was in her possession after she left prison.

In the last entry of the diary, the diarist writes: 'My dear Bunny knows all. I do not know if she has the strength to kill me. I pray to God she finds it . . .'

What is interesting about this entry is that he refers to Florence by her pet name, and calls her 'my dear'. Yet throughout most of the diary, she is referred to as 'the whore'.

On 29 March, the day of the Grand National, Florence met Brierley, and went arm in arm with him to see the royal party. Maybrick was furious. Only a week earlier, she had been committing adultery with Brierley, and there seems no doubt that her husband suspected what had happened. And when he and Florence arrived home after the Grand National, he blacked her eye. Florence immediately decided to leave him. The following day she went to see the family doctor, Arthur Hopper, and told him that she was going to see a solicitor to try to get a separation. Hopper went to Battlecrease House later the same day, and made strenuous efforts to reconcile them. He later wrote that he had effected a 'complete reconciliation'.

The discovery of the body of Elizabeth Stride,
one of Jack the Ripper's victims

Elliott O'Donnell's book *Great Thames Mysteries* (1929) contains a chapter called 'Was it Jack the Ripper?' It begins: 'In May 1887 began a series of mysterious crimes which, for barbarity and almost superhuman cunning, have rarely been equalled and certainly never surpassed.'

He describes how two men pulled a bundle out of the river at Rainham, in Essex, and found that it contained the trunk of a woman of about twenty-eight, with the head, arms and legs missing.

On 8 June 1887 another parcel was found in the Thames near Temple Stairs and proved to contain some of the limbs that belonged to the previous body. More remains found in Regent's Canal, Chalk Farm, also proved to belong to the body. At the inquest, the pathologist declared that the limbs had been severed by someone with a knowledge of anatomy.

On 11 September 1888 – the year of the Jack the Ripper murders – a left arm was found in the Thames near Pimlico, and two weeks later, another left arm in the grounds of the Blind Asylum at Lambeth.

The next find was in New Scotland Yard itself, which was then in the process of being built. A workman who went into the basement to recover his tools – which he kept hidden behind some boarding in a recess – noticed a black bundle, also in the recess. When he and an assistant manager took it out into the daylight, they discovered it was a human torso with the head and arms missing. It was wrapped in woman's black silk dress.

A further search of the basement, this time with a sniffer dog, revealed a leg and a foot belonging to the same body. The pathologist commented that the foot seemed exceptionally well-shaped, and probably did not belong to a woman of the working class.

Two police doctors agreed that the arms already found belonged to the same body. One of them was of the opinion that the hands again showed a woman who was not used to manual labour.

The speculation in the newspapers that this dismemberment was the work of Jack the Ripper led to a letter to the Central Newsagency – to which previous ripper letters had been sent – in which the writer, who signed himself 'Jack the Ripper', swore solemnly that the victim found near the Thames had nothing to do with him. He went on to promise another triple murder – which never took place.

Does this explain why the diarist refers to her as 'my dear Bunny' instead of 'the whore'?

In any case, Florence may have had another reason for wishing to have a 'complete reconciliation' with her husband. There were rumours that she was pregnant when she went into prison, and that this was the reason that the death sentence was commuted to life imprisonment. Some months later, a newspaper report showed a picture of her sitting in the prison nursery holding a baby.

If Florence was pregnant by Alfred Brierley, then she had a very good reason for wishing to be reconciled to her husband. She had to make him believe that he was the father of the child who would be born in less than nine months' time.

If this is true then it disposes once and for all with the suspicion that Florence murdered her husband. A woman who has gone to the trouble of trying to deceive her husband into believing that he is the father of her illegitimate child is not planning to murder him in a few weeks' time.

If the Maybrick diary is genuine, then it provides the most positive proof so far that Florence Maybrick was innocent of poisoning her husband.

Chapter Five

New Light on
Lizzie Borden

The Lizzie Borden case is undoubtedly America's most celebrated unsolved murder.

In summary, the facts of the case are as follows. On 4 August 1892, on one of the hottest days of the year in Fall River, Massachusetts, thirty-two-year-old Lizzie Borden screamed for the maid, telling her: 'Someone's killed Father!' Seventy-year-old Andrew Borden, a banker, was lying dead on the settee, his head and face destroyed by hatchet blows. A search soon revealed that his wife Abby – Lizzie's stepmother – was also dead in the spare bedroom – it was later established that Mrs Borden had died about ninety minutes before her husband, who had been killed some time around eleven o'clock.

Lizzie claimed that she had been out in the barn, looking for some lead weights for a fishing-line – she intended to go off the following morning to the seaside town of Marion to do some angling. (Her sister Emmy was away staying with friends.) The only other person staying in the house was an uncle called John Morse.

Three days after the murder, Lizzie burned one of her dresses declaring: 'It's all covered up with paint.' The possibility that she had destroyed a bloodstained dress naturally made her a prime suspect.

After the inquest, at which Lizzie admitted that she did not call Mrs Borden 'Mother', she was arrested and charged with murder.

LIZZIE BORDEN.　EMMA BORDEN.　REV. MR. BUCK.　MRS. C. J. HOLMES.　MR. C. J. HOLMES.

THE PRISONER AND HER FRIENDS IN COURT.

Lizzie Borden in court

89

Her trial began ten months later, on 1 June 1893, at New Bedford, Massachusetts. But it was obvious from the beginning that the evidence was purely circumstantial, and there was nothing whatever to connect Lizzie with the murders. Thirteen days later, she was acquitted.

Since then, there have been a stream of books on the case, most of them assuming her guilt. The first book to take the contrary view was Edward D. Radin's *Lizzie Borden: The Untold Story*, published in 1961. Radin concluded that the murderer was the maid, Brigitte Sullivan.

Six years later, Victoria Lincoln, who was born in Fall River, produced a new theory in her book *A Private Disgrace*. According to Victoria Lincoln, Lizzie Borden murdered her stepmother because she was furious about a property deal. Five years before the murder, Andrew Borden bought a house belonging to his wife's brother and sister, and gave half of it to Abby. Lizzie felt that charity should begin at home, and stopped calling Abby 'Mother'. According to Victoria Lincoln, Andrew Borden was about to do the same kind of thing again on the day of his murder. Uncle John Morse – the brother of Borden's first wife Sarah – asked if he could rent a farm belonging to Andrew Borden. Once again, Borden decided to transfer the farm into his wife's name. Victoria Lincoln believes that Lizzie murdered her stepmother to prevent this deal going ahead, and may have killed her father because she realized that he would be horrified – as he certainly would – that she was a killer.

In 1992, David Kent's book *Forty Whacks, New Evidence in the Life and Legend of Lizzie Borden*, reviewed all the evidence, including a great deal that had not been publicized earlier, and demonstrated conclusively that, whether Lizzie was guilty or not, she should certainly never have been accused of the murder and brought to trial.

'Without a plausible motive (or, with a decidedly weak one, even if proved), without a weapon or the surely

It happened in the Priory, Balham, south London, where Charles Bravo, a thirty-year-old barrister, lived with his newly married wife Florence. She was an attractive girl, who had been a widow for four years when Bravo married her in December 1875. Her first husband, Captain Alexander Lewis Ricardo, of the Grenadier Guards, had died of alcoholism, leaving Florence a welcome – and, she thought, well-earned – £40,000.

When Charles Bravo proposed to her, he was aware that she was the mistress of a middle-aged doctor called James Manby Gully, who had tended her when her first marriage was breaking up. Charles's sexual past had not been entirely blameless, so the lovers agreed to put all thoughts of jealousy from their minds. Charles was undoubtedly in love with her, and just as undoubtedly attracted by her money.

As she soon discovered, he could be overbearing and bad-tempered; but Florence wasn't the type to be bullied. She had a mind of her own – and a tendency to drink rather too heavily. She ran the Priory – an imposing Gothic pile – with the help of a widow named Mrs Cox. To begin with, the marriage seemed happy – even though Florence had two miscarriages in four months, and Bravo suffered from fits of retrospective fury about Gully, and once even struck her.

On Friday, 21 April 1876, Charles Bravo ate a good supper of whiting, roast lamb, and anchovy eggs on toast, washing it down with burgundy.

Florence and Mrs Cox drank most of two bottles of sherry between them. At ten that night, loud groans came from Bravo's bedroom; he had been seized with severe abdominal pains, and began vomiting. He vomited for three days, until he died.

Sir William Gull, Queen Victoria's physician (who was suspected by some twentieth-century crimonologists of being Jack the Ripper), saw him before he died, and gave his opinion that Bravo was suffering from some irritant poison. A post-mortem confirmed this – there were signs of antimony poisoning. At this point Mrs Cox declared that Bravo had told her: 'I have taken poison. Don't tell Florence.'

An open verdict was returned at the inquest. But the newspapers smelled scandal, and openly hinted that Florence had killed her husband. Another inquest was held, prompted by Charles's brother Joseph, who was out to get a verdict of wilful murder – which would lead to Florence's arrest.

This time, the Dr Gully scandal came into open court – doing Gully a great deal of professional damage. Added to this, a dismissed servant of the Bravos' testified that he had once bought tartar emetic for the doctor. But again, the jury decided that there was not enough evidence to charge anyone – although they agreed that it *was* a case of murder. So Florence was exculpated, and she died of alcoholism two years later in Southsea.

Ever since then, students of crime have argued

about the case. The most popular theory, obviously, is that Florence did it. An inquest on the body of her first husband – conducted after the Bravo inquest – showed traces of antimony in his organs. However, Ricardo had by then been separated from Florence for months.

It seems possible that his violent attacks of vomiting were not due to alcoholism, but to slow poisoning with antimony. But why should Florence kill her husband? Possibly because he insisted on his marital rights, and she was terrified of further miscarriages; possibly because she came to realize that he was interested only in her money.

bloodstained clothing, and without that prime requisite, exclusive opportunity, the case against Lizzie was simply not a case at all. They had obtained an indictment that held a busted flush for a hand. They could prove nothing.' His own view is that a woman of Lizzie's Christian upbringing and impeccable social history could never had committed murder with a savagery so evident in the Borden case.

Kent's book certainly establishes that there was no real evidence against Lizzie, and that the case would probably not even have reached a modern court of law. But he ends by admitting: 'What is the truth of what took place at 92 Second Street? It is the eternal enigma. The story will forever remain unfinished. Perhaps Lizzie was the only person who knew the truth.

'Perhaps not.'

David Kent died shortly after his book was finished, and so allowed him no chance to comment on a book published in 1991, *Lizzie Borden, the Legend, the Truth, the Final Chapter*

Florence Bravo

New Light on Lizzie Borden

by Arnold R. Brown. In this book, Brown undertakes to name the real murderer.

Arnold Brown was also born in Fall River – in 1925. He admits that he had always taken Lizzie's guilt for granted. But after his retirement to Florida, he met a man named Lewis (Pete) Peterson, also of Fall River, and when they were discussing Ted Kennedy and the Chappaquiddick mystery, the name of Lizzie Borden was mentioned, and Peterson commented: '"That one is no mystery either. My father-in-law knew the killer."

"You mean Lizzie?" I asked smartly.

"Hell no. I mean the guy who killed them!"'

Peterson then explained that when his father-in-law, Henry Hawthorne, was eighty-nine years old in 1978, he wrote down his story of what really happened. Peterson allowed Arnold Brown to read this account of the case.

Henry Hawthorne's father had been a poor tenant farmer of a man named William Borden, the son of Deacon Charles L. Borden.

William Borden's 200 acre farm contained large orchards, and part of his income came from the cider he made. But he also made applejack – that is, allowed the barrels of cider to freeze, so that the alcohol retreated to a small space deep inside the ice, then drilled through the ice, and tapped the almost pure alcohol, which was, in effect, apple brandy. Borden consumed large quantities of his own apple brandy, and as a result, spent a great deal of his time less than sober.

Borden was a strange, wild man, and in some ways the small boy – Henry Hawthorne was six years old when he first met him – found him terrifying. To begin with, Borden was the local slaughterman hired to put down horses and other animals, which he did with a single effective swing of an axe. Borden loved his axe so much that he seldom left his farm without carrying it in a coarse homespun satchel. The first time Henry Hawthorne met him, Borden playfully chased him with the hatchet, so that the terrified boy trembled for hours afterwards. But when the boy had overcome his fear, they became friends. According to Hawthorne he was about eight years old when he realized that William Borden was mentally about the same age. 'Bill had just one toy, year in and year out: his hatchet, which was always close at hand. Henry played boys' games with his toys: Bill chopped, cut and killed things with his. Whenever they sat and talked boy talk, Bill produced a whetstone and stroked the blade edge of his hatchet with a sensual rhythm impossible for an eight-year-old to understand.' Bill Borden told Henry that his hatchet had been his only friend until Henry's family moved there.

One day, Bill Borden made the child drunk on applejack. He found the first mouthful horrible, but soon got used to it. Later he was violently sick.

According to Hawthorne, Borden told him that the deacon was not his real father – he had adopted Bill at a very early age. The deacon and Bill both knew the identity of the real father, but no one else did. Many times, Borden repeated that his real father was dead.

One day, when Borden was drunk on applejack, and the child had also taken a few mouthfuls, Borden began to talk to his hatchet. 'You knew my father and that fat sow he married when he should have married my mother. Of course you knew them: you were there when they died!'

When Henry Hawthorne grew up, he became a succesful salesman, and left his life of poverty behind. He married a girl called Mary Eagan, whose mother, Ellan Eagan had walked past the Borden house on the morning of the murder. His mother-in-law seemed to be extremely interested in his stories about William Borden, and freqently asked him questions – such as what kind of a bag Borden used to carry his hatchet in. She was also interested in one of her son-in-law's stories about a practical joke that Borden had once played on him. After they had cleaned out the cider barrels with some special mixture concocted by Borden, Borden gave him a substance that looked like axle grease, and told him to be sure to rub this grease on any part of the body that had been in contact with the barrel cleaner. Hawthorne did this, and soon afterwards began to smell so appalling that even the livestock would not come near him. He described the smell as a mixture of boiling horsemeat, rotting apples, rotten egg and a touch of skunk, and added that even that mixture would be perfume to the smell of the 'axle grease'. It lasted for about three days. Later, he was told about a horse disease called Blister Beetle Poisoning (Blister Beetle is another name for Spanish Fly), and the stench it left behind in the dead horse's bladder. The vet who told him about this said that anyone who got some of this substance on his own skin would be shunned by the rest of the human race for days until it wore off. Hawthorne was convinced that this was the stench that was given off by the axle grease.

One day, his mother-in-law asked him whether Borden had owned a 'duster' (a long overcoat) of the same material as the bag he carried his hatchet in. Hawthorne asked with astonishment how she knew about it. Borden had always worn his 'duster' – made by his wife – ever since the day when a piece of horse butchery had gone wrong, and his best suit was covered in blood. In fact, his aim was usually so accurate that he split the horse's skull with a single blow, and almost no blood drained out.

Ellan Eagan eventually told him why she was so curious. On the morning of the Borden murder, she had passed by the house at about ten o'clock, and seen the maid Brigitte outside cleaning the windows – as had several other people. But when she passed the Bordens' backyard a second time, she saw a man who was making his way towards the gate.

Murders

This man was quite distinctive, and even at a distance of several yards, smelt horrible. What struck her as strange was that, on one of the hottest days of the year, the man was wearing a kind of overcoat made of what looked like burlap – the material of which sacks are made – and was carrying a bag made of a similar material over his shoulder. The man saw her, and hesitated as if he meant to go back. He looked into her eyes for a moment, and then took a step towards her. She ran, and a moment later, rushed into the next yard to be violently sick. (It was not simply his smell – she was also suffering from what she called 'summer grippe', nausea produced by heat.)

Ellan Eagan finally decided to take her story to the police, but the constable was completely dismissive. He told her to go away and stop wasting his time. By then, the police had already decided that Lizzie Borden was guilty. When his mother-in-law told him this story, Henry Hawthorne realized with a sudden shock that Bill Borden had been telling the truth when he said to his hatchet: 'Of course you knew them. You were there when they died!'

This, then, is the story told by Arnold R. Brown. He spent two years attempting to research it. William Borden's mother was called Phebe Hatharway, and he was forty-five when he died – an apparent suicide – in 1901. That meant that he was born in 1856. Brown succeeded in getting hold of the birth certificates of several of the children of Deacon Borden, but although he was able to trace three daughters and two sons, neither of the sons was called William S. Borden. It looked as if Deacon Borden and his wife had recorded the births of their children, all except William. Brown learned that there is an old law in Massachusetts that means that birth certificates of illigitimate babies are not available as public records. He believed that this explains why he was unable to trace William Borden's birth certificate.

New Light on Lizzie Borden

When William Borden died in April 1901, the Taunton *Daily Gazette* reported his death with a note that he was 'undoubtedly insane' and that he had spent a period in the local asylum a few years before. Brown immediately directed enquiries to the Taunton State Hospital. He received two replies, both stating that they were unable to trace the relevant file, although they *did* have a card for William S. Borden that listed the names of his sisters. Yet after this apparent admission, the same official sent Brown a letter claiming: 'We do not have a record of admission to this facility, at all, ever. If he had been here, we would know.'

Brown began to feel that, for some reason, an official embargo had been placed on all records of William Borden.

When he studied accounts of Borden's death in the local newspapers, he began to suspect that perhaps it was not suicide after all. Borden had apparently drunk a six-ounce bottle of carbolic acid, then climbed a tree in the dark before dawn, tied a chain around his neck, and either jumped or fallen off the branch. His neck had been broken. Another odd fact was that Borden was wearing his best clothes. Brown concluded that it sounded a good deal more like murder than suicide, and that possibly he had been disposed of by some of the same authorities who were so anxious to keep details of his life a secret.

Brown's belief – which he does his best to justify on some rather slender evidence – is as follows.

Lizzie and her sister were, he believes, fully aware that they had a half-brother. He points to a peculiar little exchange at the inquest. The District Attorney, Hosea Knowlton, asked her: 'How many children has your father?'

'Only two,' Lizzie answers.

'Only you two?'

'Yes, sir.'

Murders

'Any others ever?'

'One that died.'

Is Knowlton hinting here that he knows about the existence of William, the bastard son? If not, why is he so persistent about such an unimportant matter?

Brown believes that William Borden – who would then have been in his mid-thirties – came to see his real father that morning, perhaps to discuss some kind of cash settlement. Brown speculates that he may have entered the house before midnight the previous day, and possibly even slept in Emma's empty bedroom. Or he may have spent the night in the hayloft of the Borden barn. Brown suggests that William Borden was waiting in the guest bedroom when Mrs Borden walked in to change the sheets. Possibly they had some conversation – Borden explaining why he was there. At all events, Brown believes that the psychopathic William Borden killed her with his hatchet, and left her in the position in which she was found, virtually crouching on all fours with her head on the floor.

Lizzie had left her bedroom at about nine o'clock that morning, shortly before her father left the house to go down-town. While he was out, Lizzie busied herself with various household chores like ironing handkerchiefs. Her father returned home at 10.45. He was tired – he and his wife had been violently sick the day before – and he now sat down on the settee and dozed off to sleep. According to Lizzie, she then went out to the barn to look for the fishing weights – in another version of the story, she went and ate pears outside under the pear tree. In the quarter of an hour or so that she was away, William Borden came downstairs, and killed his father. This murder was, of course, necessary – since Borden knew that his illegitimate son was in the house, or was coming to meet him that morning.

Having killed his father, William Borden hastened into the yard. The photograph of the Borden house included in

New Light on Lizzie Borden

Edmund Pearson's *Trial of Lizzie Borden* shows that there was only a narrow gap between the house and the fence – perhaps three feet. So Ellan Eagan, walking past on the other side of the fence, could have been as close as a foot away from the man in the strange overcoat.

But why did Lizzie Borden not name her half-brother as a suspect? One possibility, of course, is that she had no idea he was anywhere near the house at the time of the murder. Brown's theory is that it was connected with the will. We know that Andrew Borden had made a will in which he left Lizzie and her sister $25,000 each – a fairly small sum when compared to the bulk of his fortune, which was over a million dollars. This has often been cited as a reason why Lizzie killed her mother and her father. Brown believes that as soon as Lizzie realized that her mother and father were dead, and suspected that the culprit was her half-brother, she also realized that she had a very good reason for keeping silent. If she denounced William Borden, then it would become general knowledge that he was her half-brother, and that Andrew Borden was his father. He would become eligible for one third of Andrew Borden's estate. Even if he was convicted of murder, his third of the estate would probably go to his wife. If, on the other hand, Lizzie kept silent, then she and her sister would share the estate – which is, in fact, what happened.

The next part of Brown's theory is more difficult to follow. He is convinced that Fall River was run by a kind of cabal which he calls, the 'Silent Government'. He says that in many small towns and cities in America, most of the municipal jobs – including the police force – were in the hands of a small number of men of influence, the doctors, judges, lawyers and other members of the upper middle class. He explains – without explaining how he knows – that the Silent Government established a kind of command post in the Mellon Hotel in Fall River. He further believes that this 'Mellon Hotel gang' also knew that William Borden was the real culprit, but that they agreed with Lizzie that neither he nor his family should benefit from the murder. So, according to Brown, it was a question of allowing a murderer to go free in order to make sure that Lizzie and her sister shared Andrew Borden's vast fortune. Brown seems to believe that the motive was partly financial – that they expected to be 'paid off'. And he cites the fact that when Emma died, she left an estate valued at half a million, while Lizzie's estate (on her death in 1927), was worth less than half that. He thinks that the significant exchange between District Attorney Knowlton and Lizzie at the inquest – about how many children Andrew Borden had – was intended to signal to Lizzie that he knew perfectly well about the existence of her half-brother.

Brown also believes that another murder, that of a twenty-two-year-old girl named Bertha Manchester, which took place ten months later, was also committed by William Borden. Bertha Manchester was hacked to death with a hatchet on the morning of 31 May 1893, not long before Lizzie's trial opened. The hired man, Carrero, was accused of the murder. According to the medical examiner, she was struck about the head and shoulders in the same locations as Abby Borden. Carrero waited on the property – according to the prosecution to kill Bertha's father – and was later arrested. He always protested his innocence, but was institutionalized as 'criminally insane', and released after twenty-five years, after which he was deported back to the Azores. Brown believes that the jury sentenced him to an institution rather than to death because there was some doubt about his guilt. Brown appears to suspect – although he does not say so – that William Borden might even have committed the murder to make sure that his half-sister was acquitted.

But, according to Brown, Lizzie's acquittal had already

In 1930, an American actor called Philip Yale Drew came close to being hanged for a murder he did not commit.

At 6.15 on the evening of Saturday, 22 June 1929, Mrs Annie Oliver returned to the tobacconist's shop where she had left her husband, Alfred Oliver, serving a customer. She found him dying behind the counter, and when she asked him what had happened, he said: 'My dear, I don't know.' He died twenty-four hours later.

There were no clues, and two months later, the investigation had dragged to a halt. Then, in August, Chief Constable Thomas Burrows was having a drink in the Wellington Club, opposite the Royal County Theatre when another member commented to him: 'That chap you're looking for is Yale Drew, the actor fellow who was in *The Monster*.'

Drew was arrested in Nottingham, where his company was acting, and a pair of his trousers – apparently bloodstained – was taken away. A woman who had been standing near Oliver's shop, in Cross Street, insisted that she had seen Drew wiping blood from his face shortly after the time of the murder. Drew insisted that he did not even know where Cross Street was. When another witness said that they had heard him say he was going to Cross Street to get a newspaper, Drew insisted that what he had said was that he was going 'across the street' to get a newspaper.

Two witnesses who said they had seen him near the shop were taken to Nottingham, and asked to pick out Drew as he walked along the street. Both of them did so. But then, Drew was extremely well known in Reading, so this proved nothing.

The inquest – which was, in effect, Philip Yale Drew's murder trial opened on 9 October 1929, in the Small Town Hall. It was obvious that the evidence against Drew was entirely circumstantial – people who claimed they had seen him, or someone like him, near the scene of the murder. But things began to swing in Drew's favour when a butcher's assistant named Alfred Wells came to give his evidence. He had formerly told the police that, on the day of the murder, he had seen a man resembling Drew in Cross Street – a man who carried his raincoat across his shoulder, as Drew did. But when a journalist named Bernard O'Donnell introduced Wells to Drew, Wells immediately said that this was not the man he had seen. He had spoken to him, and the man had a north country accent. He declared that he had told the police that the man he had seen was not Drew.

The police denied this – and then were forced to withdraw their denial when Wells's statement was found among a pile of papers.

The jury brought in a verdict of murder by person or persons unknown, and Drew walked out of the court a free man.

The solution to the mystery almost certainly lies in the fact that Saturday 22 June was always referred to in Reading as Black Saturday, because it was the day that the town was invaded by race gangs attracted by the annual Ascot and Windsor

> race meetings. It seems more likely that the
> unknown killer of Alfred Oliver was among these
> louts and roughs than that he was a well-known
> actor with two bank accounts, both in credit.

been decided on well in advance, with her agreement. She
would stand trial for the murder, providing a kind of
scapegoat, provided it was guaranteed in advance that she
was acquitted.

All this part of Brown's theory sounds highly dubious.
The most convincing part is obviously the testimony by
Henry Hawthorne concerning William Borden – and his
mother-in-law's statement that she saw Borden emerging
from the house at the time of the murder. It is possible, of
course, that all of this was some kind of fantasy invented
by Henry Hawthorne, who had heard some rumour to
the effect that William Borden was Andrew Borden's
illigitimate son, and made up the rest of the story. This,
admittedly, is unlikely, as is the possibility that Ellan
Eagan also made up her story about seeing a man with a
peculiar smell emerging from the Bordens' house. On the
other hand, there is no independent documentation for
any of the 'facts' in the book. There is nothing in the
police files to support Ellan Eagan's story about her
attempt to report the man in the long overcoat. There is
no evidence that William Borden was the illigitimate son
of Andrew Borden. Even if William Borden told Henry
Hawthorne that his real father was Andrew Borden, this
may well have been fantasy. Fall River was full of
Bordens – no less than 125 families – and Andrew Borden
was one of the few who were wealthy. William Borden
may simply have envied him because they had the same

name, and created a fantasy in which Andrew Borden was his real father.

Brown is also inclined to minimize or ignore some of the evidence against Lizzie. A few days before the murder, she tried to purchase some prussic acid. Brown makes the unlikely suggestion that she wanted it to defend herself against William Borden – he does not make it clear how she intended to administer it. Brown also ignores the fact that Lizzie seems to have told at least one deliberate lie that morning – when her father came in, she told him that her stepmother had received a note saying that someone was sick, and had left the house. As far as we know, this is pure fantasy. Then, of course, there is the question of the dress that Lizzie burned a few days later, claiming it was covered with paint. Was this dress really bloodstained, and had Lizzie concealed it inside one of her other dresses in her wardrobe?

On the other hand, if a search of Massachusetts Records can finally produce evidence that William Borden was really illegitimate, and if some other evidence about his fondness for wielding a hatchet could be unearthed – for example, from the records of the State Hospital – then William Borden would certainly emerge as the chief suspect in the murder of Andrew and Abby Borden.

Chapter Six

The Gorse Hall Murder

The Gorse Hall Murder is one of the oddest mysteries of the century. On the evening of 1 November 1909, an industrialist named George Henry Storrs, together with his wife, and their niece, Marion Lindley, were sitting in the dining room when the cook burst in, exclaiming: 'There's a man in the house!' She said that a moment or two before she'd seen a man standing behind the kitchen door. She thought he was the coachman, and said: 'Oh Worrall, how you startled me!' But the man pointed a revolver at her head and shouted: 'Say a word and I shoot!' She had ignored him and run straight into the dining room.

Storrs, who was large and powerfully built, rushed into the passageway, and encountered a slightly built man with a blond moustache. He grabbed him and began to struggle with him. Mrs Storrs, as she ran into the passageway, heard the man say: 'Now I've got you!' Mrs Storrs rushed upstairs, and grabbed a shillelagh that was kept on the wall, and as she raised it in the air, the man shouted: 'I won't shoot!' She snatched the revolver from his hand. Unfortunately, he proved also to have a large knife in his pocket. Storrs shouted to his wife to ring the alarm bell. Meanwhile, Marion Lindley had run out to find help.

Storrs pushed the intruder into the scullery and locked the door. A few minutes later, the man smashed the glass pane in it with a milk can and climbed through. He hurled himself again on Storrs, brandishing the knife. When the women returned, a few moments later, they found Storrs lying on the ground with several stab wounds, and no sign of the intruder.

The revolver proved to have no firing pin, but was of a peculiar type known as a 'Bulldog'.

Mrs Storrs had set off the alarm bell, and an insurance agent named Richard Ashworth came into the house in time to bend over the dying mill owner.

'Can you tell me who has done this?'

Storrs shook his head and mumbled: 'No.' Not long afterward, he died.

The police connected the murder with an incident that had taken place two months earlier. On Saturday, 10 September, at about 9.30 in the evening, a voice outside the dining-room window shouted:

'Hold up your hands, or I'll shoot!' A shot was fired, followed by the sound of breaking glass as the barrel of a gun was smashed through the window-pane. Storrs was about to rush outside, but his wife clung on to him. When, finally, they made a check of the grounds, the man had disappeared. This was why the alarm bell was installed at Gorse Hall, which was not far from the town of Dukinfield, Yorkshire.

At the inquest on Storrs, Marion Lindley told the coroner that she had heard Mrs Storrs mention the name of two men whom Storrs regarded as enemies. She wrote these names on a piece of paper, but they were not divulged to the public.

Eleven days after the murder, on 12 November, Worrell, the coachman, committed suicide by hanging himself in the stable. He was thought to be depressed at the prospect of losing his job when the Hall closed, as well as by the death of his master.

By 20 November, the police had made an arrest. It was a young man named Cornelius Howard, and Marion Lindley identified him as the man she saw struggling with her uncle. The only difference was that this man had no moustache.

The cook, Mary Evans, was not quite so certain as Marion Lindley, but she said she thought it was the same man.

Cornelius Howard, who was Storrs's cousin, was committed for trial on a charge of murder.

The trial took place in March 1910, at the Chester Assizes, before Mr Justice Pickford. Howard was described as an Artillery Reservist, thirty-one years of age. When Mrs Storrs was asked if she could see the murderer in court, she pointed at Howard in the dock and exclaimed: 'There is the man!'

Marion Lindley also identified Howard as the man she had seen.

According to Howard, he had an alibi. He had left the army in the previous April, and admitted that he had been tried – and acquitted – for shopbreaking in Sheffield. He claimed that after that, he went to a place called Joyce's Lodging House in Stalybridge, and he was there on the evening of the murder. A lodging housekeeper named Alice Doolan, from Oldham, said that Howard had come to her house on the night of the murder and played cards until the next morning. A fellow lodger of Howard denied that Howard had been in the lodging house on the evening of the murder – he said he had been away for at least two days. There was also a certain amount of conflicting evidence given by other witnesses. But what probably most strongly influenced the jury was the fact that Storrs knew his cousin perfectly well, and had not identified him. Everything that had happened suggested that he did not know his assailant. Howard was found Not Guilty.

Five months later, the police made another arrest, this time a man named Mark Wilde. They had found several witnesses who swore that the Bulldog revolver belonged to Wilde. On the night of the murder, Wilde had returned

home with bloodstains on his clothes, and told his mother
that he had been in a fight. The police also discovered that
he had owned two more revolvers, but that he had
dismantled them and disposed of the pieces – he admitted
that this was in case he was suspected of the Gorse Hall
murder. Wilde was charged with killing Storrs, and his
bloodstained jacket and trousers were sent to the forensic
analyst Doctor William Wilcox. Wilcox was able to say that
the stains were definitely of human blood, but since Wilde
had already admitted this, it made no real difference to the
outcome. Once again the jury decided that the evidence was
inconclusive. Mark Wilde was acquitted, and the Gorse
Hall mystery remains unsolved.

In fact, it seems fairly certain that Storrs knew the identity
of the man who stabbed him, although he denied it as he lay
dying. He had told the police that he had no idea of the
identity of the man who had rammed the gun through the
window in September. Storrs claimed that after he heard
the words: 'Hold up your hands or I'll shoot', and the crash
of the breaking window, he had raised the blind and seen a
revolver pointing at him. But this story has some obvious
flaws. Would the man shout 'hold up your hands' when he
couldn't see the family behind the drawn blind? Would
Storrs have raised the blind after a shot had been fired
through the window? If the man intended to kill Storrs,
why did he not fire a second shot? It sounds as if Storrs
made up the story – and fired a shot through his own
window – to provide a plausible reason for asking for police
protection. Why did he not tell them the true reason?
Presumably because he preferred to keep it to himself. Did
his wife and niece know the true reason? That also seems
unlikely; but they probably believed whatever Storrs chose
to tell them.

During the next seven weeks there had been a police
guard at Gorse Hall, and the alarm bell had been installed.

Mary Sophia Money was an attractive girl who earned her own living working as a dairymaid. In September 1905, she was living at 245 Lavender Hill, Clapham, and was not known to have any men friends. On Sunday, 24 September 1905, she told another dairymaid she was going out for a little walk. She called in the nearby sweet shop at seven o'clock and said she was going to Victoria. At eleven that night her body was found in the Merstham Tunnel, near Merstham, on the Brighton line. She had been badly disfigured by the train and had apparently been pushed or fallen out in the tunnel.

A signalman at Purley Oaks said that, as a train had passed, he had seen a couple struggling, and the man seemed to be trying to force the girl onto the seat.

No one ever discovered the name of the man Mary Money was going to meet at Victoria, or why she allowed herself to be persuaded to get on the train for Brighton. But it seems that, whoever he was, they began to argue on the way to Brighton – perhaps whether she should stay the night with him – and he pushed her out of the carriage.

Mary Money's brother, Robert Henry Money, was a dairy farmer who lived a double life. He had affairs with two sisters, and had two children by one of them, and one by the other (whom he married). In 1912, seven years after his sister's death, he took both women to Eastbourne, shot the women and the three children, and then shot himself and set fire to the house with petrol. One of the women succeeded in escaping.

Some writers on the mystery have suggested that Robert Money may have had something to do with the death of his sister, but no connection between the two tragedies was ever found.

On the night of the murder, the guard was withdrawn because there was a local election, and all police were required for keeping order. Whoever killed Storrs seems to have known this, and chose his opportunity. As he burst into the dining room, he shouted: 'Now I've got you.' He was a man with a grudge, and most writers on the case seem to agree that the likeliest reason for the grudge was that Storrs had seduced some millgirl – perhaps the man's wife or sister. Whatever the reason, Storrs chose to die without naming his assailant.

It seems a pity that Doctor Wilcox omitted one essential test. He had shown that the stains were of human blood, but he evidently did not know that there was also a test for determining the blood group of a stain. There was abundant blood on Wilde's jacket, and there must have been bloodstains at the Hall (even if these had been cleaned up, a blood sample could have been taken from Storrs's body before his burial). If the stains had been of the same blood group, it would certainly have increased the circumstantial evidence against Wilde. As it is, we only know that Storrs took to the grave the secret of why he was murdered.

Chapter Seven

The Strange Case of Hilary Rougier

The murder of Hilary Rougier remains officially un-solved. In fact, the name of the murderer is fairly obvious. But the story is sufficiently strange to be worth retelling.

Hilary Rougier was a retired Guernsey farmer, a quiet man whose bank account contained the enormous sum (for those days) of £6,000. Rougier made the acquaintance of a young married man called William Knight Lerwill, and moved in with the couple as a paying guest. He seems to have been with them for about seven years. In 1926, the Lerwills moved into a house called Nuthurst, in Lower Knaphill, near Woking. By this time, Rougier's health was poor enough to need a live-in nurse.

On 23 July 1926, Rougier felt so ill that the local GP, Doctor Brewer, was called in. His opinion was that, for a man of seventy-seven, Rougier was in good health with nothing worse than slight bronchial trouble. Mrs Lerwill, a strong-minded young lady, did all the talking. Brewer prescribed a cough mixture and left. On 6 August, Brewer saw Rougier again, and thought his condition was about the same. Then, on the morning of 14 August 1926, Brewer received an urgent phone call saying that Rougier was very ill. He arrived to find the old man unconscious, with a very feeble pulse. According to the Lerwills and the nurse, he had been perfectly all right the previous night. Brewer came to the conclusion that Rougier had suffered a cerebral haemorrhage. Later that same morning, Rougier died and Brewer signed his death certificate, certifying the cause of death as senile decay and a cerebral haemorrhage.

Rougier's solicitor was suspicious. Rougier's bank account contained less than eighty pounds. Lerwill admitted freely that Rougier had made them a number of presents, one as much as a cheque for £1,850, which had been paid into Mrs Lerwill's account.

The solicitor passed on his suspicions to Rougier's married sister and niece, who agreed that the circumstances of Rougier's death deserved investigation. They learned that Doctor Brewer had never seen his patient alone – Mrs Lerwill was always present and did all the talking. She had requested that the body should be cremated, although in fact it was buried in St John's churchyard in Woking. Yet, for some strange reason, the police ignored all this, and it was not until two years later that the Home Office finally gave permission for the body to be exhumed.

The task was passed on to Sir Bernard Spilsbury, who superintended the exhumation on 16 March 1928, accompanied by a local policeman, Superintendent Boshier. Four years earlier, Spilsbury had worked with Boshier on the poisoning of Alfred Jones, the landlord of the Blue Anchor Hotel in nearby Byfleet, for which a Frenchman named Pierre Vaquier was hanged.

Spilsbury stood by the side of Doctor Brewer as the grave was opened – a situation he found intensely embarrassing since he knew how easy it was for a general practitioner to make a wrong diagnosis in the case of an old man. His embarrassment was justified for in the morgue, it was revealed that Rougier's brain showed no sign of a cerebral haemorrhage, but that most of his other vital organs contained large quantities of morphine. The fact that there were still traces in the body more than eighteen months after his death meant that there must originally have been a considerable quantity, since morphine tends to disappear as a corpse decays.

Now Nuthurst had previously belonged to a certain Doctor Hope, who died there, and his daughter had let the house to the Lerwills. It contained Doctor Hope's drug cabinet, but this was locked and she had the key. The medicine cabinet proved to contain a bottle of laudanum (an opium derivative containing morphine) which was half empty. The bottle was graduated in sixteen divisions, and at the inquest – at which Spilsbury and Doctor Roche Lynch gave evidence – Lynch explained that five divisions would have been a fatal dose. Moreover, although the medicine cabinet was locked, it had a defective hinge, which would have enabled anyone to get into it without a key.

William Lerwill was asked about the cheque for £1,850; he agreed that only the signature was Rougier's, and that he had made out the rest of it. Mrs Lerwill claimed that she had nothing to do with money matters.

A strange incident occurred during the inquest. After the summing up, a messenger brought in an envelope, with Lerwill's name written on it. William Lerwill opened the envelope, took out a single sheet of paper, and collapsed in a faint, breaking the chair as he fell. When someone looked at the paper, it proved to contain a drawing of a gallows, with a man hanging from it underneath which were the words 'you are the murderer'.

But although the jury brought a verdict of death by morphine poisoning, not self-administered, the Lerwills were allowed to walk out of court – after all, there was no evidence that they had administered it. And they could always point to the presence of the nurse in the house as evidence that they would have lacked the opportunity.

Two newspapers were rash enough to hint that they thought Lerwill guilty of murder, upon which he sued them

On 30 September 1906, a young British woman named Madeleine Lake, was found murdered in a wood near Essen, Germany. The money in her purse was still intact, so she was carefully examined for signs of sexual assault. There were none.

Four months later, in February 1907, a twenty-year-old clerk named Alfred Land walked up to a policeman and said he wanted to give himself up for the murder of Madeleine Lake. His story was that he and two companions called Karl and Heinrich had grabbed Madeleine Lake with the idea of sexual assault, but became alarmed after she lost consciousness. All three had run away to Belgium, but he had come back to give himself up. He had no idea of what had happened to the other two.

In court in Essen, he admitted that the two companions were a figment of his imagination. But just as it seemed that a guilty verdict was absolutely certain, a woman who kept a café at Essen where Land always took his meals insisted that he was there both at lunchtime and in the evening at about 7.30. She proved the date by an entry in an account book. Her two daughters supported her story.

Land's sister told how he had attempted suicide after their father died of tuberculosis and alcoholism. She said that her brother was also an alcoholic. He had been in prison a number of times for fraud.

So, in spite of his protests that he was guilty and wanted to be executed, Land was found Not Guilty.

The evidence suggested that Land had made a

false confession to a murder he did not commit out of a desire for notoriety.

But the killer of Madeleine Lake was never caught.

and obtained £5,000 in damages. Thereupon, he walked out on his wife and child, and went to Canada.

In 1933, Lerwill returned in haste to England, leaving behind him a string of dud cheques. In March 1934, he moved into a hotel in Combe Martin called the Pack o' Cards (so called because it was built by a local squire who had made a fortune playing cards).

Lerwill was strolling along the street when he was approached by the local constable, who knew he was a stranger, and simply meant to make him feel at home by having a chat.

'How long are you going to stay in Combe Martin?' asked the constable.

'A few days longer I hope,' said Lerwill. Then he made the curious comment: 'But should we be walking along together like this?' The policeman looked at him in surprise and said: 'Why not?'

As they were strolling along, Lerwill noticed a newspaper on display, with a large front-page photograph of a man called Reginald Hinks being led along by a prison warder. Hinks was a vacuum-cleaner salesman who had moved in with a widow called Constance Fallen who lived with her eighty-five-year-old senile father. In December 1933, Hinks called the fire brigade to say that he had found Mr Fallen with his head in the gas oven, and had pulled him out. 'If you find a bruise on the back of his head,' said Hinks, 'that was made by me as I was pulling him out.' However, medical examination proved that the bruise was made before death, and Hinks was charged with murder.

For some reason, the picture of Hinks unnerved Lerwill, and he made the strange remark: 'I want to talk it over with you.' Before the policeman could ask him what he meant, he darted behind a small car that was parked by the pavement, reached into his pocket, pulled out a small bottle, and drank something from it. By the time the policeman reached him, he was already dead. The bottle had contained prussic acid.

Two months later, on 4 May 1934, Reginald Hinks was hanged for the murder of James Pullen.

Chapter Eight

The Black Dahlia Murder

The murder of Elizabeth Short – known as 'The Black Dahlia' because of her jet black hair and the rumour that she always wore black underwear – has always created the same kind of morbid fascination in America as the Jack the Ripper murders in England.

On 15 January 1947, a boy walking his bicycle shortly after dawn saw a battered black car draw up on a piece of waste ground on Naunton Avenue, Los Angeles. He noticed casually that one of the mudguards was spattered with mud, and that there were dents along the passenger side. But he was on his way to a newspaper round, and paid it no more attention.

At about 10.30 that morning a young housewife named Betty Bersinger was pushing her three-year-old daughter in a pram along Naunton Avenue when she noticed something white ahead of her, rather like someone lying on the waste ground at the edge of the pavement. An outstretched arm and leg made it look like a store window mannequin. It seemed to have broken in the middle. At this point, Betty Bersinger noticed a sort of red bobble on one side of the chest, and realized that it was a part of a breast. It was at this point that she realized that she was looking at the corpse of a young woman.

She hastened to the nearest house, knocked on the door, and told the woman who answered that she had to call the police. Minutes later, officers Will Fitzgerald and Frank

Perkins headed towards the waste ground on Naunton Avenue. They found a shocked-looking youth waving his arms at them. He pointed.

'That's a dead woman...'

The girl was lying among the weeds, and the body had been cut in half at the waist, with the two halves separated by a space of about a foot. Her legs were spread apart, and her arms bent at right angles and raised above the shoulders. Someone had sliced through both corners of her mouth, enlarging it grotesquely almost to the lobes of her ears. There was no sign whatever of blood around the wounds or around the body. It seemed to have been drained completely and then washed before being dumped there.

Nearby, on the pavement, there was a cement sack with spots of watery blood.

The opinion of Lieutenant Jeff Haskins, who arrived a few minutes later, was that this was what he called a 'defiance killing', a sex crime that was deliberately intended to shock.

The head of the crime lab, Ray Pinker, thought that the body had been placed in the lot somewhere before early dawn; the upper torso had been put there first, face down, then turned over. After that the lower torso had been carried from a vehicle on the cement sack. His guess was that the bruises on the head and lacerations to the face suggested that she had been attacked with some blunt instrument that caused her death. He estimated that she had been dead for about ten hours. Strangely enough, the girl's black hair – which was red in places – appeared to have been washed or shampooed after she was dead.

The fingerprints of the corpse were taken, and led to her prompt identification, her name was Elizabeth Short, and she was twenty-two years old. She was born in Hyde Park, Massachusetts, on 29 July 1924, was five feet five inches in height, weighed 115 pounds, and was a brunette

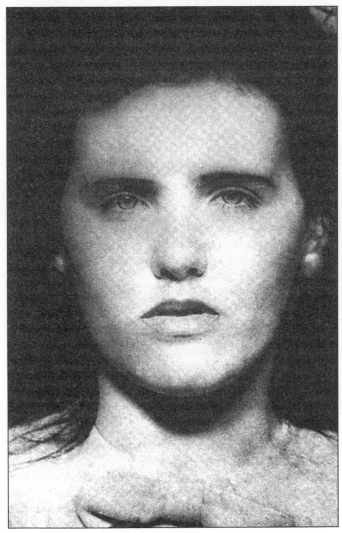

Elizabeth Short, the Black Dahlia

with blue eyes. (Her black hair turned out to have been dyed.)

In the Los Angeles County Morgue, the examiners were puzzled by the position of the lower half of the body. It seemed to be bent upwards at the hips, as if she had been in a semi-recumbent position when she was killed and rigor mortis had set in. When they attempted to take the temperature by inserting a thermometer in the rectum, this proved to be impossible – although the entrance to the rectum was dilated, there appeared to be some kind of obstruction. With a pair of forceps, one of the examiners finally removed several pieces of flesh. These had obviously been inserted into the dead girl and looked as if they had been cut or gouged from her left thigh.

Later that day, police surgeon Newbarr recorded that the body was 'that of a female about fifteen to twenty years of age. There are multiple lacerations in the mid forehead, in the right forehead and at the top of the head in the mid line. There are multiple tiny abrasions, linear in shape, on the right face and forehead. There are two small lacerations, one fourth inch each in length, on each side of the nose near the bridge. There is a deep laceration in the face three inches long which extends laterally from the right corner of the mouth. The surrounding tissues are ecchymotic and bluish purple in colour.

'There is a deep laceration two-and-one-half inches long extending laterally from the left corner of the mouth. The surrounding tissues are bluish purple in colour. There are five linear lacerations on the right upper lip which extend into the soft tissue for a distance one-eighth inch.'

Her teeth proved to be in an advanced stage of decay and one lower incisor was loose.

The left breast had not, as at first appeared, been partly removed, but only cut into.

One of the most startling discoveries came when Newbarr opened her stomach. It contained 'fecal matter' – that is to say, excrement. This had apparently been forced into her mouth, and she had been made to swallow it.

Whoever had killed Elizabeth Short was either a violent sadist, or had some reason for hating her.

As soon as the body had been identified by its fingerprints – which were on file from a job application at an army base near Santa Barbara – reporters on the Los Angeles *Examiner* succeeded in getting through to Elizabeth Short's mother, on a neighbour's telephone. She was not told immediately that her daughter was dead – the reporters wanted to get as much information out of her as possible before she went into shock. So Phoebe Short was told that her daughter had won a beauty contest, and that the *Examiner* was calling because they wanted some background for a story about her. Phoebe Short said that her daughter Elizabeth – known as Beth – had come to Los Angeles hoping to get into films. After that, she proceeded to read aloud a letter which she had recently received from Pacific Beach. At this point, the reporter interrupted, and admitted that Elizabeth had been murdered, and that the *Examiner* was going to do everything in its power to make sure that justice was done. Phoebe Short was not told any of the horrible details.

She was obviously shocked. She wanted to know if this was a joke, and then said that she would not believe it until the police came and told her so. After that she hung up. The reporter who had been talking to her went out and got drunk.

As a result of that story, the *Examiner* that day sold more copies than at any time in its history except for VJ Day. In the 1980s, a Los Angeles reporter named John Gilmore would research Elizabeth Short's brief life. This is what he discovered.

Her father had been a skilled mechanic who owned a garage in the small town of Wolfbro, not far from Boston. At first, they prospered. Elizabeth was the third of five sisters. Then came the depression of 1929, and suddenly, Cleo Short's business was deeply in debt. One day, he abandoned his car on the Charlestown Bridge and vanished. It looked as if he had killed himself. Elizabeth – then known as Betty – was shattered, and in a single year missed thirty-six days of school. She began to suffer from asthma. Their mother had to support the family by working six days a week as a clerk in a bakery in nearby Medford.

The eldest sister Virginia was a talented musician, and often listened to opera on the radio. Betty would quarrel with her about this – she preferred popular music.

When she was sixteen, Betty's mother arranged for her to stay with friends in Miami Beach, Florida, and Betty spent most of the winter there. Her asthma disappeared in Florida. She returned home in the spring, but for the next two years, went back to Florida every winter. By the age of eighteen, Elizabeth Short was beautiful, with a figure like a model, and a gentle smile. She worked as an usherette in a cinema.

At about this time, Phoebe Short received a letter from her husband Cleo, who was in Northern California. He admitted that he had been unable to face his money worries, and had simply deserted his family. His excuse was that if he appeared to be dead, his wife might be eligible for more support. He told her that he would like to return home. She lost no time in replying that he could stay away.

Betty, on the other hand, was delighted to hear that her father was still alive, and wrote to him in Vallejo, California. He replied that he was working at Mare Island Naval Base and invited her to come and stay with him. Phoebe Short was against the idea, but Betty insisted. She arrived in California in 1943, at the age of nineteen.

The reunion with her father was not the ecstatic event she hoped for. She was full of ambition – she hoped to become either a model, or a film star. Her father had been a working man for several years, and his wife's refusal to take him back had made him bitter. Within a few weeks, it had become clear that father and daughter had very little in common. Elizabeth was untidy, and liked to spend most of her time in cafés and bars. She dated sailors from Mare Island, and her father angrily accused her of being lazy and having 'bad morals'. Finally, she was forced to leave.

A soldier drove her to Camp Cook, north of Los Angeles (now Vandenburg Air Force Base) where she succeeded in getting a job. It was here that she decided she wanted to be called 'Beth' rather than Betty. She was hired as a cashier in the canteen.

The soldiers on the base found her fascinating, but it was soon general knowledge that, where sex was concerned, she kept men at arm's length. Because the base was overcrowded, there were no quarters immediately available for her, and she was sleeping wherever she could find a spare bed. A sergeant invited her to move into the spare bed in his trailer, but when she rebuffed him, gave her a black eye. After this, she was moved into quarters with a WAC sergeant.

She went on to win a beauty contest as 'the Camp Cutey of Camp Cook'. But the accommodation problem on the base finally drove her to look elsewhere. The soldier who had driven her to Camp Cook had told her to look him up in Santa Barbara – also north of Los Angeles. There, she was sitting in a restaurant with an obstreperous group of soldiers and girls when the manager called the police. Since she was still under age, she was charged with being a minor in a place where liquor was served.

A policewoman named Mary Unkefer took pity on her and put her up until she could be sent back to Boston. Her father was contacted, but said he wanted nothing more to do with her.

So Beth Short returned to Boston, went down to Florida again, then finally, bored with jobs as a waitress, once more made her way back to Los Angeles. She telephoned a friend called Sharon Givens, who was in Houston, Texas, asking her

> During Elizabeth Short's early days in Hollywood,
> she visited a fortune teller on Hollywood
> Boulevard with a friend called Marjorie Graham.
>   Marjorie recalled later that Beth Short had been
> in high spirits before they went to the fortune
> teller, but that when they left the gypsy, she
> seemed 'saddened and uneasy'. 'Whatever that
> woman told her had disturbed Beth. She seemed
> to have other things on her mind the rest of the
> day and was depressed.'

to lend her some money. Throughout her short life, Beth Short
was prone to borrow money from friends and acquaintances.
Sharon telegraphed her a money order to the Clinton Hotel in
Los Angeles. There, Beth shared a room with a girl called
Lucille Varela, and the two spent a great deal of time in cafés
and bars. Lucille was to comment: 'Beth wore so much make-
up it was really hard for anyone to tell how young she was.'
Beth began to spend her days trying to find work at the
Hollywood Studios. She ended by taking a job at the
Hollywood Canteen, a place frequented by servicemen, with
a friend called Barbara Lee, and there met an Air Force pilot
named Gordan Fickling, with whom she went out on a
number of dates.

One day in the Formosa Café near the Goldwyn Studios, the
actor Franchot Tone tried to pick her up. He tried his favourite
line when she said she was waiting for someone, he said: 'Of
course, you're waiting for me.' He name-dropped about
directors and other film stars, and told her that he could get
her an interview for a job in films. When Tone invited her up to
an unoccupied office, with a bed in a back room, he was
convinced that he had made a conquest. But when he tried to
kiss her, she rebuffed him, and was obviously disappointed

that he only had 'that' in mind. It seemed that, when she realized the price she was expected to pay for her interview, she decided against it. Tone was upset by her disappointment. He gave her his phone number and a few dollars, and called a cab for her. Unfortunately, she never took advantage of the meeting – Tone might have been able to help her find work.

As it was, she agreed to pose for an artist called Arthur James, and did not demur when he asked her to pose in the nude. She even seems to have agreed to pose naked with another woman for a painting called 'Sappho'.

She was shocked when one of her fellow hostesses at the Canteen, a daughter of wealthy parents named Georgette Bauerdorf, was murdered in her apartment off Sunset Strip. Georgette was found floating face downwards in the bathtub on 12 October 1944. She was wearing only a pyjama-top. In the other room, the bottoms of her pyjamas were found, torn down the side, and there was a bloodstain on the floor.

At first, it was assumed that she had slipped and fallen into the bathtub, until the doctor examining her realized that she had a piece of towel jammed into her mouth. Her jaws were clenched so tight that it was impossible to pull it out. It had obviously been pushed into her mouth to stop her screaming, and had suffocated her. After that, she had been raped.

Her car was missing, and the following day was found in downtown Los Angeles. The killer had evidently driven it away.

Georgette's family intervened to prevent publicity – newspapers were already reporting that she was a 'good time girl' whose address book indicated that she dated many servicemen, who came back to her apartment.

Beth Short was so shocked by the murder that for a while she refused to go back to the Canteen. She was also upset because Gordan Fickling had been shipped overseas.

Soon she lost her job as an artist's model. James was arrested in Tucson, Arizona, that November. He had gone to a hotel with Beth Short and a girlfriend called Bobbie Harris, and had bought both girls presents – with cheques that were fated to bounce. When Bobbie admitted that she had had sexual intercourse with him during the previous night, he was arrested, charged with violating the Mann Act – transporting a woman across a state line for immoral purposes. The act was aimed at preventing white slave traffic, but in 1944, America was still a rigidly moral country where any kind of immorality could cause problems. In due course, Arthur James was sentenced to two years imprisonment. Beth went on to Chicago, then back home to Medford.

On New Year's Eve 1945 she fell in love again. Another Air Force Officer, Major Matt Gordon, asked her to marry him.

She also renewed acquaintance with a man named Phil Jeffers, whom she had met in Chicago, and he often took her out for meals. When he confided to her that he was still a virgin, she told him that she was too. But she went into his room in a rooming house where women were forbidden, and they would take off their clothes and give each other Swedish massages. 'We stayed virgins,' said Phil Jeffers later.

He was also to note that she obviously had some secret troubles. One evening, her face suddenly became sad. When he asked her what was wrong, she refused to tell him.

A few days after VJ Day – 14 August 1945 – she received a telegram from Matt Gordon's mother. It informed her that Matt had been killed in a plane crash on his way back from India. Her response was to write to Matt Gordon's mother asking if she could lend her enough money to start a new life. After that, she once again established contact with Gordan Fickling. He sent her a hundred dollars to come out to Long Beach, south of Los Angeles. But when she got there, she was disappointed to learn that Gordan was simply hoping that she would become his mistress. He was not interested in the idea of marriage. Her reaction was to begin to date other servicemen in Long Beach.

It was about this time that she acquired the nickname 'the Black Dahlia'. The Alan Ladd film *The Blue Dahlia* had just been released, and two soldiers who knew Beth started to call her the Black Dahlia. This, apparently, was because she wore a black two-piece beach costume. But other room mates would also testify to the fact that she preferred to wear black underwear.

She was soon back in Los Angeles, sharing rooms with girlfriends, and again accepting many casual dates. The account of one of her men friends of that period makes it clear that she was not, as many writers have asserted, an 'easy lay'. Martin Lewis was the manager of two shoe shops, and soon noticed Beth looking in the window almost every morning. He was married with three children, but could not help noticing how attractive she was. One day, she came in and asked to try on a particularly expensive pair of shoes. But she made excuses about buying them, and he guessed that she had no money. One day, she accepted his suggestion to go out to lunch. They went to a local cafeteria, and when she mentioned that she had left her purse locked in her apartment, he lent her enough money for her car fare back. A few days later, she came back into the shop and returned the car fare. She tried on the shoes again, then asked if she could pay for them later, because she needed the money to join the Movie Guild. As she asked him, he noticed that the slit in her dress was open to the top of her garters. She asked: 'Do you like what you're seeing?' and he admitted that he did. 'Would you like to see some more of me?' He asked her to return to the shop at closing time.

There, in his car, he handed her the shoes in a shoe box. After this, she cuddled against him, putting her head on his shoulder. They drove to a quiet place, and began kissing. He unzipped his trousers and put her hand inside. Then, as she leaned forward, he pushed her head down, and she performed oral sex. Afterwards, she cleaned him up with a handkerchief, and he took her back to her hotel. As she left the car, she whispered that she cared for him.

After this, she came into the store a number of times, and he gave her, at different times, three pairs of shoes, as well as giving her money for her rent.

The next time they were in the car, he tried to persuade her to have sex, but she explained that it was her period. He tried to persuade her to allow him 'to do it the other way', she refused, but allowed him to pull her dress up around her waist. Finally, he had to be content again with oral sex.

Next time she came in, he took her into the stockroom to show her some new shoes, and asked her to raise her dress. She explained that it was again her period. He said that he didn't mind. She then took his hand and pushed it down the front of her skirt, into the waistband of her panties, while holding on to his wrist. He noted that it was like 'touching a child, because there was basically very little to feel'. It seems that Beth Short had very little pubic hair, and that her labia were undeveloped. After this, she allowed him to touch her breasts, and he gave her the shoes and a handbag.

It seems clear that, while Beth Short was willing to offer men a certain amount of satisfaction, she held them to strict limits.

One day, a friend of Martin Lewis told him that he had seen Beth Short in a pornographic film. He went to see it in the friend's office, but was inclined to doubt whether the black-haired girl who was performing oral sex on a dark-skinned man was Beth Short. He was inclined to think that the black hair was a wig. And when he later remarked jokingly that he had heard she was in a 'stag' movie, she laughed and asked if he thought that *she* would do something like that.

Many men would later describe their acquaintance with Beth Short at about this period. She seemed to have a naive,

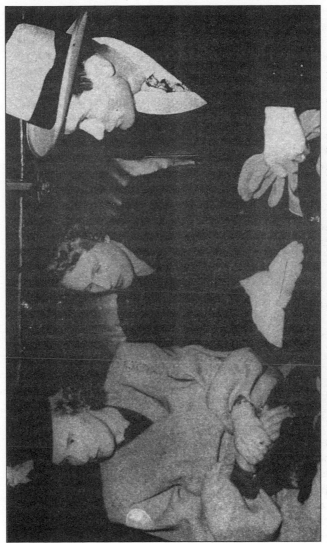

Elizabeth Short's mother and sister on their way to Los Angeles to identify the mutilated body

open quality about her – the quality that was to turn Marilyn Monroe into a sex symbol. In fact, Marilyn Monroe – two years Beth Short's junior – was also in Hollywood at this period, leading much the same kind of life as Beth Short, doing her best to become a film star, and diffusing the same vulnerable charm.

Through a girl called Ann Toth, Beth met a nightclub owner named Mark Hansen, who suggested that she should move into his house, where there were already a number of aspiring young actresses waiting for parts. She preferred to move into a cheap room – costing a dollar a day – which she shared with three other girls. One of them noticed that she sometimes took an hour to make up her face, while another commented that with her black hair, white make-up and bright red lipstick, she made herself look like a Chinese doll.

Towards the end of 1946, she was finding it increasingly difficult to pay her rent and her other bills. Quite suddenly, she left Hollywood and went south to San Diego. She borrowed twenty dollars from a friend to get there.

In San Diego, she went into an all night cinema, and fell asleep. A twenty-one-year-old cashier named Dorothy French woke her up in the early hours of the morning, when Beth was the only person left in the cinema. When Beth told her that she had nowhere to stay, Dorothy invited her back to her home. There she was introduced to Dorothy's mother Elvera and her younger brother Cory.

Dorothy French's account of the three weeks that Beth Short spent in their house offers a clear picture of her personality. Most days, she slept until after eleven. She stayed out until two o'clock in the morning, explaining she was with a prospective employer. She went back to the cinema where Dorothy worked, and spent most of the night out with the manager. Later, she accepted his invitation to go back to his house, and came back with scratches on her arms, which she said had happened while he was grabbing her. From then on, she saw the manager – or some other man – almost every night. Beth was the kind of girl who found it easy to pick up men – Dorothy noticed that, even as they walked along the street together, men would stop and stare after her. Elvera French even became worried because her fourteen-year-old son was so obviously smitten by Beth, while Dorothy was slightly annoyed that Beth tended to use him as an errand boy. He even offered to let her move into his bedroom, while he would sleep on the settee.

'She'd talk about her Hollywood connections while painting her toe-nails or putting on make-up. Often she'd use cold cream to take it off and then start all over again . . . She used a jar of cold cream I had, and then asked if she could use my mother's Noxzema.'

What emerges from Dorothy French's account is that Beth Short was vivacious, kind, sweet, but somehow vague, self-absorbed and disconnected. Her mind was always on bright dreams of the future, never on the present.

Just before Christmas 1946, Beth was picked up by a travelling salesman named Robert Manley. The newly married Manley was driving through San Diego when he saw her standing on a corner. He went around the block and passed her again, this time offering her a lift. After some hesitation, she finally accepted. When he asked her if she was married, she said no, then changed her mind and said yes – her husband was an officer who had been killed in the Air Force.

He drove her back to the Frenchs' house, then asked her to have dinner with him. After this, he drove to a motel and rented a room for two.

They stopped for drinks, but when he suggested going for a meal, she said she would be contented with sandwiches – she was not very hungry. They stopped in a cafeteria for a hamburger and a sandwich. Finally, at one o'clock in the morning, he drove her home – deciding against asking her back to his hotel room for a nightcap. She allowed him to kiss her goodnight, and he went back to his motel room.

She had written to Gordan Fickling for money, and he sent her a hundred dollars. But he also seems to have told her that their relationship was at an end. On Christmas Eve, she told the Frenchs that she was going to have dinner with a young man, and did not return until late on Christmas Day – with presents for everyone.

During the next week, Beth seemed to be in a state of depression and uncertainty. On New Year's Eve, she became drunk at a nightclub and passed out – her date brought her back early the next morning. She slept until noon, then spent the rest of the day in a Chinese dressing gown, talking with Dorothy and her mother.

There was an odd incident: two people, a man and a woman, came to the door and knocked. They could see another man waiting in the car. Beth became frightened and asked them not to answer the door. Finally, the three people drove away.

On 7 January, she received a telegram from Robert Manley – who called himself 'Red' because of his red hair. He told her that he was coming back to San Diego. It seems to have been at this point that she decided to leave the Frenchs and return to Los Angeles. When he arrived in San Diego on 8 January, her suitcases were packed, and he put them in the back of his car. They went to a hotel that had a band, and there he noticed that she kept glancing towards the door as if waiting for someone. They went on to a nightclub, and they danced and had more drinks. When they left, she suddenly announced that she wanted to take a bus for Los Angeles. They went to a cafeteria and bought hamburgers, then went back to his motel room. Suddenly, she seemed intensely tired, and sat with his overcoat around her shoulders. When he asked her if she was coming to lie down and try to get some sleep, offering to sleep in the armchair, she said: 'No, you sleep on the bed.' He climbed into bed, closed his eyes, and suddenly fell fast asleep. He woke up in the morning and found Beth sitting up on the other side of the double bed, propped against a pillow. When he looked at his watch, he realized that he was going to be late for his first appointment.

This occupied most of his morning, while Beth stayed behind in the motel room. Finally, some time after midday, they headed back to Los Angeles. There, she told him that her sister lived in Berkeley, and was married to a college professor named West. Her sister, she said, was going to meet her in Los Angeles, at the Biltmore Hotel. They arrived late in the afternoon. He put her suitcases into a luggage locker at the Greyhound Bus depot, then they went to the Biltmore. The desk clerk said that no Mrs West had rung up. Manley explained that he had to be getting back home.

After Manley had left, Beth Short sat in the lobby for a long time. Finally, she got up and went out. The doorman saw her walk down towards the Greyhound Bus Station. It was the evening of 9 January 1947. Five days later, her body was found on the weed-covered lot. What happened to her during the next four days has never been established.

The murder of Beth Short threw the Los Angeles Police Department into a turmoil. Everybody wanted action. All kinds of horrifying rumours were soon circulated – Beth Short had been tortured for four days before death, she had been suspended upside down and burned with cigarettes. In fact, she had been stabbed many times with a short-bladed knife – never deeply enough to kill her. Someone had forced her to swallow excrement. But the bruises on her face showed that she must have been half-unconscious at the time. She had probably lapsed into unconsciousness from loss of blood after a short time. The murder was bad enough, but it was not as bad as rumour suggested – and as a number of writers have since stated in print.

Detective Harry Hansen soon learned about the telegram from Robert Manley, and Manley was brought in for questioning. The questioning was so severe and exhausting that he collapsed after taking his second lie detector test. Years later, his wife was to claim that the police questioning had caused him to have a mental breakdown. (In fact, Manley had had some psychiatric problems before he met Elizabeth Short.)

More than 150 sex offenders were interviewed within days of the finding of the body. Cranks and attention-seekers confessed to the murder. Within a few months the number had reached twenty-eight – but the police were able to eliminate all of them. A few questions quickly revealed that they had no real knowledge of the crime.

Beth Short's cases were retrieved from the Greyhound Bus Station. They revealed that she had a taste for expensive clothes, and for black underwear, otherwise they offered no clues.

Six days after the body was found, a man called the editor of the Los Angeles *Herald-Express* telling the editor that he intended to give himself up, but that first he wanted to have a little more fun 'watching the cops chase me some more'. Before he hung up he said: 'You can expect some souvenirs of Beth Short in the mail.'

A few days later, in the mail box of the Biltmore Hotel, the postman discovered a brown paper parcel addressed to the 'The Los Angeles *Examiner* and Other Papers'. Underneath this, letters cut out of newspapers read: 'Here is Dahlia's Belongings, Letter to Follow.' The package proved to contain an address book with the name of Mark Hansen stamped in gold on the cover, Elizabeth Short's birth certificate and her social security card and a number of photographs of her. The address book contained dozens of names, but several pages had been torn out. All these items had been washed with petrol to remove possible fingerprints, and although it had evaporated, it could still be smelt. The police painstakingly interviewed everybody whose name was in the book,

Lynn Martin, former flatmate of the Black Dahlia
taken in for police questioning

tracking some of them across the United States. Once again, they reached a dead end.

Almost two years later, police were still interviewing suspects. A Miami bellhop named Dylan wrote to Dr Paul de River, a consultant psychiatrist to the Los Angeles Police Department, and an expert on sex murder – to tell him that he had worked with a friend called Jeff Conners in Los Angeles, and that Conners had known Elizabeth Short. He thought that Conners might be able to help in the investigation. Rivers telephoned Dylan, and sent him his air tickets to come to Las Vegas, offering to let him help on a book he was writing on sex crime. They met at Las Vegas, and it soon became clear to Dylan that he had been lured there because he was a chief suspect in the investigation. He was refused a request to contact his wife or his lawyer, but succeeded in dropping a card in the street addressed to Los Angeles lawyer Jerry Giesler, asking for his help. Giesler received the card, and was able to secure Dylan's release. Dylan's friend Jeff Conners was also arrested and grilled about the murder, but was able to prove an alibi. Dylan was so bitter about his week in custody that he sued the City of Los Angeles for $100,000. As a result, the Los Angeles Police Department came in for a great deal more harsh criticism, and suggestions that it should be investigated for corruption.

During the course of the next few years, the police continued to receive occasional false confessions. Crime writers produced their own theories about the Black Dahlia's murderer. One writer of fiction, James Elroy, produced a gruesome novel called *The Black Dahlia* (1987) in which the murderer proves to be a sadistic woman. (It had been suggested at the time that Elizabeth Short's killer might have been a jealous lesbian.) Ramona Sprague is a fat and unattractive woman, trapped in a loveless marriage with a Scottish contractor. The contractor's younger brother is obsessed with dead things, and Ramona poisons neighbourhood cats for him. She also seduces him, and bears him a child. When her husband sees a resemblance between the child and his younger brother, he slashes his face horribly, turning him into a kind of monster. Elizabeth Short is involved with the brothers, making pornographic films. It is Ramona who knocks Elizabeth Short unconscious with a baseball bat, forces the 'monster' to tie her up, then spends several days torturing her to death.

In fact, the Los Angeles Police Department had held documents suggesting the identity of Elizabeth Short's killer since the late 1950s. These were finally unearthed by a journalist named John Gilmore, son of an officer in the Los Angeles Police Department. In his book *Severed, The True Story of the Black Dahlia Murder*, John Gilmore offers the first convincing solution to the mystery of Elizabeth Short.

The murderer, according to Gilmore, was an ex-convict named Jack Anderson Wilson, who used many aliases, including Arnold Smith.

Some time in the early 1960s – Gilmore is unfortunately vague about the date – the Los Angeles Police Department learned that 'a certain individual' wanted to talk to them about the Black Dahlia murder. The informant – who is not named – offered the Los Angeles Police Department a tape which had been made by a man called Arnold Smith, in which Smith describes how an acquaintance named Al Morrison, a female impersonator, had murdered Elizabeth Short.

What convinced the detectives was one detail that was not publicly known. Elizabeth Short had an undeveloped vagina, so that sexual intercourse was impossible. This had been verified by a doctor she consulted in Chicago. Elizabeth Short was incapable of promiscuity, because her physical abnormality prevented her from satisfying males.

According to Smith, Morrison was a sadist who enjoyed choking girls. (This is a well-known perversion – Peter

Kürten, the Düsseldorf 'Ripper', needed to squeeze a woman's throat to reach orgasm.)

Smith convinced the 'informant' of his genuineness when he brought an old candy box to a meeting place, and showed him a number of photographs, including one of himself with Elizabeth Short. The other man in the photograph, Smith claimed, was the murderer Al Morrison. Smith claimed that other things in the box – such as hairpins and a handkerchief – had belonged to Elizabeth Short.

Smith describes an occasion when he himself brought her to his hotel room. She lay down on the bed, while he sat drinking whisky. Smith said he got onto the bed and put his arm round her, turning her on to her back. He said that she seemed lifeless, like someone who had drunk herself into a stupor. When he put his hand on her breasts, she breathed 'in a real exasperated way'. He began trying to undress her, and as he wrestled with the clasp of her brassiere, she asked him not to. 'You're going to be disappointed anyway.' After that, according to Smith, he contented himself by putting his mouth against her stomach, while she lay there staring up at the ceiling.

According to the tape, 'Morrison' saw Elizabeth Short walking across Hollywood Boulevard. He invited her into his car, and drove to San Pedro Street, then he picked up a key, and took her to an empty house belonging to a Chinaman on 31st Street. The place had been closed up for a long time and smelt stale.

When she told him she wanted to go to make a phone call, he told her she couldn't. She asked if she was a prisoner and he replied: 'That's right. You're a prisoner.' She tried to leave the room and he pulled her back by the arm. She hit him with her handbag and caught him on the side of the face. 'He slugged her once and her knees got weak.' He dragged her back into the room and as she started to scream, he hit her again, then several more times. (Elizabeth Short's face was badly bruised, and her nose was broken.)

As she lay on the studio bed, he gave her a drink from his bottle. It hurt her mouth. When she tried to get up, he hit her again.

As she lay on the bed, he cut off her clothes, then stuffed her panties into her mouth. After that, he tied her up tightly with rope.

'Morrison' then stabbed her several times with a short-bladed knife, 'not enough that would kill you, but jabbing and sticking her a lot and then slitting around one tit, and then he'd cut her face across it. Across the mouth. After that, she was dead.'

Elizabeth Short was not, in fact, dead, but the obstruction in her mouth had prevented her from breathing, and she had relapsed into deep unconsciousness.

He dragged her into the bathroom, where he placed a number of boards across the bath, then laid her on these face downwards. Tying her again with ropes – the motive of tying a dead body is not clear – he decided that he had to dissect the body in order to be able to move it more easily. Then it struck him that it would be easier to cut it in half at the waist.

With a larger knife, approximately ten inches long, he sliced into the body. He was startled when blood spurted out, some of it going onto the floor. Apparently Elizabeth Short had not been dead after all. But as soon as he began to cut, the haemorrhage probably killed her instantly.

When the body had been cut in two, he filled the bath with water, then pushed both halves of the body into a sloping position above the water, so that the blood would run out. This was the reason that, when the body was found, the lower half was 'bent' at the waist, as if she had been sitting up when rigor mortis set in.

Finally, early the next morning, 'Morrison' wrapped the two halves of the body in a plastic tablecloth and plastic shower curtains, placed it in the boot of his car on a cement sack, and dumped it on the waste ground at 39th Street and Norton Avenue.

What made it quite clear that Smith had some intimate knowledge of Elizabeth Short was his comment that Morrison claimed to have had sex with her. 'You see, the first thing is you couldn't fuck her at all.'

Their informant told them that he had no idea where to find Arnold Smith. Smith would contact him occasionally, and then they would meet.

The detectives were certain that Smith was the man they were looking for. The descriptions of the murder – and often of the murderer's state of mind – was far too exact and detailed to be second-hand. They asked the 'informant' to try to set up a meeting, during which Smith would be introduced to an undercover agent from the Los Angeles Police Department. But Smith failed to call the informant. Finally, he rang him to say that he had to go to San Francisco, and would be in contact the following week.

Before that could happen, fire engines were called to the Holland Hotel, Los Angeles, where Room 202 was ablaze. When the firemen had put out the flames, they saw a charred corpse lying on the bed. The manager identified it as Jack Wilson – alias Arnold Smith – a tall, thin man – six feet four inches – who walked with a limp. Several times in the past year or two, the room had caught fire because he smoked in bed after he had been drinking heavily. That evening, he had returned to the hotel carrying bottles in a paper bag.

Research by the Los Angeles Police Department revealed that Wilson, who had been born in Canton, Ohio, in 1920, had a long criminal record, for crimes including

The murder of Evelyn Foster at Otterburn,
Northumberland, remains unsolved.

Evelyn Foster, twenty-seven, was the daughter
of a garage proprietor of Otterburn, and often
active as a hire-car driver.

On a freezing evening in early January 1931, a
bus driving over the desolate moors between
Otterburn and Newcastle passed a car that was
smouldering about ten yards from the road. The
driver went to investigate, and on the far side of
the car, found Evelyn Foster, all her clothes
burned off, in a state of severe pain. The girl was
taken to her home, and soon afterwards she
died. But in the meantime, she had succeeded in
telling her story.

That afternoon, in a village called Ellishaw, a
strange man told her that he wanted to get to
Ponteland to catch a bus to Newcastle, and at 7.30
that evening, she picked him up near Ellishaw and
drove as far as a place called Belsay. There, the
man had made some kind of sexual advances to
her, and when she refused, hit her in the eye so
hard that she lost consciousness. The man then
drove her in the car to a place called Wolf's Neck,
where it was found, and drove out onto the moor.
There, it seems, he dowsed the car in petrol, then
set it alight. She opened the door and fell out onto
the grass. She said that she saw the man go back to
the road, saw another car stop for him, and heard
a conversation before the other car drove away.

At the inquest, some puzzling contradictions
arose. Her face was not only unburned, but

unmarked – there was no sign of a black eye or a bruise due to being hit violently enough to knock her unconscious. Evelyn Foster had also told her mother that she had been 'sexually interfered with'. Yet again, there was no evidence of attempted sexual assault.

In spite of this, the jury brought a verdict of murder by person or persons unknown.

One suggestion that has been made is that Evelyn Foster accidentally set fire to herself in the process of burning the car in the course of an intended criminal fraud. There were two insurance policies, amounting to more than £1,100. But it seemed that Evelyn Foster was not in any financial trouble – she had £1,400 in the bank.

The idea that she died accidentally is also contradicted by the fact that she claimed her passenger had told her that he'd been picked up at Jedburgh by three Scottish motorists and had had tea with them. The police succeeded in locating these motorists, but they denied giving a lift to anyone that day. The killer – whom Evelyn Foster described as a small man wearing a bowler hat and a dark coat, and speaking like a gentleman, must have seen the three Scottish motorists for they actually existed. This means that he himself must have existed.

And what about the car that stopped and picked up the killer? Would the driver not be curious about the car burning a few yards away? Or did the killer claim that he had had an accident that had caused his car to burst into flame? In that case, why did not the driver of the other car come forward when the case was publicized?

Evelyn Foster's money was untouched. So the motive was not robbery. But if it was sexual assault, why did he not carry out his intention while she was unconscious? Why did he set fire to the car?

Evelyn Foster usually took a male garage employee with her when she acted as a hire car driver. Why did she not do so on this occasion, although her sister asked her to? Did she know the man who attacked her? All these questions remain unanswered.

burglary, robbery, drunkenness, violence, sodomy, and other sexual offences. He had used more than a dozen aliases, being arrested in several states, and was collecting benefit from a North Carolina social security number.

Some of the evidence suggested that Wilson had a motive in murdering Elizabeth Short. Smith was involved closely with a group of men at a place called Greenberg's Café, including the proprietor, who had taken part in a series of robberies and burglaries. Finally, the police swooped and arrested all the members of the gang except Wilson. He may have been afraid that Elizabeth Short – who had frequently seen him in company with the other gang members – might talk about it and get him arrested.

Members of the Los Angeles Police Department are also convinced that Wilson was also the killer of Georgette Bauerdorf. Gilmore mentions that he is believed to have joined the army in 1944 – although it is not clear how a man who had one leg shorter than the other came to be accepted –

and that he used the Hollywood Canteen where both Elizabeth Short and Georgette Bauerdorf worked as hostesses. The police believed that Georgette Bauerdorf was not killed by a casual intruder, but possibly someone she had dated once or twice, and perhaps even taken back to her apartment. A tall, thin man was seen outside her apartment shortly after the murder.

Why did Elizabeth Short's killer slash and mutilate her? Arnold Smith's description of undressing her on his bed helped to provide an answer. 'You're going to be disappointed anyway.' Smith knew that Elizabeth Short had a physical deformity that made sexual intercourse impossible. And when she was tired – as on this occasion – she became dull, indifferent, apathetic. For a man like Wilson, whose perverse sadistic urges awakened when he was drunk, this indifference would have been a challenge. Whether she liked it or not, he was going to possess her. So when she tried to leave the room, he beat her unconscious, then carried out the ultimate violation.

A photograph of the author bears the caption: 'John Gilmore on the lot where the house in which Elizabeth Short was murdered stood until 1960.'

Chapter Nine

The Murder of Shirley Collins

The pathetic death of fourteen-year-old Shirley Collins hardly ranks as a great murder mystery, yet it has some intriguing aspects that have never been explained.

Shirley lived in Melbourne, Australia, with foster-parents Alfred and Mavis Collins in the Melbourne suburb of Reservoir. Her mother had remarried and gone to live in Queensland, and she chose to remain with the Collinses, who had known her since she was a child. She was happy with them, but she continued to write to her mother every week.

Shirley was a pretty blonde with blue eyes and dimples. She left school at fourteen, and took her first job as a counter assistant at Coles Bourke Street store. Young males who were impressed by her looks found her timid and withdrawn. But she accepted the invitation of one of them – Gavan Willoughby – to his eighteenth birthday party on 30 August 1953. Another assistant named Ronald Holmes, who was twenty-one, offered to take her. Holmes thought that Shirley was at least eighteen. Shirley went home and asked Mavis Collins if she could go, and her foster-mother gave her permission on condition that she came back by midnight, and was brought home.

The party was in Richmond, and although Ron Holmes agreed to drive the considerable distance to Reservoir, Shirley told him that she would go to Richmond by train and meet him there, near the bridge outside the station.

Murders

Mrs Collins walked with her to the bus stop and recalled that, just before she boarded the bus, Shirley made the remark: 'I've plenty of time, Ron's not expecting me at West Richmond until eight.' It did not strike Mrs Collins at the time that Richmond and West Richmond are two entirely different places, not even situated on the same line. Shirley had gone to the wrong place.

Not surprisingly, Ronald Holmes waited and waited, and finally gave up at nine o'clock. He then went on to the party in Punt Road, Richmond. He was not able to ring Shirley because the Collinses were not on the telephone.

At midnight, Mavis Collins lay awake listening for Shirley's return, but by 3 a.m, the girl was still out. She crossed the road and knocked on the door of a neighbour, Constable Snell. Snell said that probably Shirley had stayed late at the party and decided she might as well stay the night, particularly if she'd had too much to drink. Mavis Collins was out at dawn the next day, and at ten o'clock reported to the police that Shirley was missing. They went to Gavan Willoughby's home, and then learned what had happened from Ronald Holmes. On Monday morning, Mrs Collins telephoned her husband, who was taking a short holiday at the home of a friend in south-west Victoria.

At nine o'clock on Tuesday morning, a seventy-four-year-old man walking his dog up the drive of a weekend cottage at a place called Mount Martha, thirty-eight miles from Melbourne, found a half-naked girl surrounded by dried bloodstains. He hurried down to the Mount Martha police station.

Shirley was naked up to the shoulders, and her coat and skirt had been pushed up around her head. When these were pulled back, it was seen that her skull had been completely crushed in by a blow from something

---

Practically everybody but his closest friends and a few reporters are convinced that Richard John Bingham Lucan, seventh Earl of Lucan, is a murderer. The evidence is strong that on the chilly night of 7 November 1974, John Lucan burst into the expensive London townhouse occupied by his estranged wife and children, attacked and injured his wife, and killed, probably by accident, the children's nanny, Sandra Rivett. The mystery is that Lord Lucan then disappeared, and though he was one of the most sought-after men in the world, no trace of him has ever been found.

---

like a stone or a beer bottle. The broken necks of three beer bottles, with the caps intact, were still lying nearby. After that, the killer had pulled off her shoes, stockings, and the rest of her underwear, flinging them around at random. After that, he had heaved up a section of a heavy glazed pottery drain and smashed it down on the girl's head.

The government pathologist, Doctor K. Bowden, stated that there was no sign of rape. She was still virgo intacta. In fact, there was no sign of any kind of sexual assault.

Shirley had obviously been taken there by car. The puzzle is, why had a girl as timid and cautious as Shirley got into someone's car?

A clue was provided after a radio programme reconstructed what had happened that evening. Among the many calls that came in was one from a migrant woman, who said that shortly after 8 p.m. on the evening Shirley was killed, she was walking along Hoddle Street towards North Richmond station when she saw a young girl standing on the corner. A light-coloured motorcar slowed down and sounded its horn. The girl walked across Elizabeth Street towards the car which reversed back towards her, and the girl spoke to the driver. She said that the driver seemed to be a man of about forty with a long face and fair hair brushed straight back. But the woman had to catch a train, and hurried on. So the basic facts now seemed clear. Shirley had realized that she was at the wrong station, and it seems likely that she knew the man who stopped the car. Almost certainly, conversation that followed was about how she seemed to be at the wrong station – one that did not have a bridge outside it. In all probability, the driver of the car told her that she was supposed to be at Richmond station and offered to drive her there.

This might explain why Shirley had got into a car, but it could not explain why she had then allowed the driver to take her thirty-eight miles. Perhaps he threatened her, but that seems unlikely. A famous Aborigine tracker named Charlie, a kind of human bloodhound, studied the footprints around the body, and announced that the girl had not struggled – she had climbed out of the car and led the way up the dark drive until the man struck her down from behind. For the first few yards, she had been so far ahead of the man that she could easily have run away into the bushes. Evidently, she trusted him. Yet she knew perfectly well that the party she was invited to was not thirty-eight miles away. The fact that the man was carrying beer bottles suggests that he told her that he was on his way to a party. But that still fails to explain why such a timid girl went with him – apparently willingly.

Subsequently, four men confessed to Shirley's murder, but all of them proved to be cranks.

Nine months after Shirley's death, in June 1954, Inspector H. R. Donelly, who was in charge of the investigation, told a magazine called *Truth*: 'We have been very close to our man a number of times. We know it and so does he . . .' *Truth* commented: 'The process of breaking down an alibi is slow, police point out, but the murderer knows continual investigations are whittling away his chances of escape.' But apparently this hope came to nothing. Questions about Shirley's disappearance – including the motive – still remain unanswered.

Chapter Ten

Who Killed
Serge Rubinstein?

The death of Serge Rubinstein is a mystery only in the sense that there are far too many suspects. There can be few businessmen of the twentieth century who have had so many enemies who wished them dead.

At 8 a.m. on 27 January 1955, Rubinstein's English butler knocked on his employer's bedroom door at 814 Fifth Avenue, New York. When there was no reply, he went in. The room was in chaos. And the master of the house, dressed in midnight blue silk pyjamas and bound with curtain cord, lay in the middle of the carpet. His face had been badly beaten, and medical examination showed that he had been strangled.

Rubinstein had been a small, chubby man about five foot seven inches tall, with a squeaky voice and an explosive enthusiasm. His greatest hero was Napoleon Bonaparte.

Rubinstein was one of the most successful businessmen of his era. When he died, he was worth more than ten million dollars. Most of this had been acquired by trickery, skullduggery and downright fraud.

In his autobiography Rubinstein explains how, when he was ten years old – in 1920 – he had helped his parents flee from Russia by leaving in advance with his fur coat stuffed with rubies, diamonds, emeralds and sapphires, and with securities packed into his trousers. According to Rubinstein, his troika was pursued across the ice by furious Bolsheviks, but reached Finland safely. A few months later, his parents and his elder brother André joined him in Stockholm. They were living in Vienna when Rubinstein turned fifteen, and when asked what he wanted for his birthday, he astonished everybody by saying that he would like to be psychoanalysed by Doctor Alfred Adler. The reason, he explained, was that he was afraid of developing an inferiority complex.

According to Rubinstein, Adler dismissed him after three sessions with the words: 'If I cure you, you'll be just ordinary. The way you are now, you'll be driven by ambition and desires.'

Rubinstein's ambition was certainly stimulated by the fact that his father died a bankrupt in the Balkans. He persuaded his elder brother André to finance his education at Cambridge, and when he was told that he needed to learn Latin, settled down and mastered it in a few months. Typically, he failed to repay his brother the money he borrowed for his education, and made possibly his first life-long enemy.

His professor of economics at Cambridge was John Maynard Keynes, who apparently told him that he was destined to be 'one of the world's financial figures'. So, at the age of twenty-three, Rubinstein succeeded in finding himself a job as the manager of a small bank called the Banque Franco-Asiatique in Paris. But he had no intention of remaining in that position. The bank was the financial agent of General Chiang Kai-shek, who at that time appeared to be winning in the long struggle against Mao Tse-tung. The Chinese had defaulted on an earlier bond issue, but the bank had launched another bond issue for them, and warned them that their credit depended upon meeting interest payments. Quietly, Serge Rubinstein bought up the earlier bond issue for a mere $25,000. When the Chinese forwarded a million dollar payment on the new bonds, Rubinstein lost no time in impounding it and pocketing the money. 'I just paid myself off,' he explained blandly.

Over the next four years, a number of equally dubious

Murders

Cambridge professor and author, John Maynard Keynes

deals swelled his fortune. But finally the French government grew tired of him. He had heard of a chain of restaurants worth $450,000, but, because of financial problems, it would be possible to get control of them for a mere $60,000. Rubinstein purchased the restaurants, and then used their assets in a series of speculations on the international money markets. He made a fortune – more than a quarter of a million dollars – but caused the value of the franc to fluctuate wildly. In 1937 the French decided to deport him.

In London, he moved into the Savoy Hotel, and prepared to take advantage of a British Mining Company – the Chosen Corporation – that he had gained control of before he left France. Now, using information from a paid informer, Rubinstein leaked to the financial press the story that the managing director was selling its stock illegally. The corporation's stock slumped, and the managing director, now threatened by legal proceedings, sold Rubinstein 173,000 shares to meet his legal expenses. Instead of paying him, Rubinstein told him that the money had been deposited in the Paris bank. The director went to jail, and Rubinstein bought up another 150,000 shares at rock bottom prices. The mining company that he had hijacked was worth $6,000,000.

Rubinstein hurried off to Japan, in company with his latest mistress, a beautiful Hungarian who called herself Countess Natasha, and sold the Korean mine to a conglomerate headed by Japan's Prince Ito for $3.5 million paid in yen. There was one condition – the money had to stay in Japan, whose economy in 1937 had been hit by a Chinese boycott. Rubinstein used his influence to convert two million dollars of it into sterling, and smuggled out the remaining two million in notes in the wide belts worn by the Japanese women he hired for the occasion. The result was that the Japanese currency lost a third of its value.

The former shareholders of the Chosen Corporation sued Rubinstein for their money. When the case was heard, the court had to follow an incredibly intricate process in which assets were shuffled back and forth between four Delaware companies, four New York companies, three Texas companies, four British companies, and one Japanese company. In some strange way, most of the assets of the company had vanished in this complex operation. Although it cost Rubinstein a million and a half dollars in legal fees, he still ended with a clear two million dollar profit.

In 1938, Rubinstein had moved to the United States. He succeeded in doing this by declaring himself a Portuguese subject named Serge Manuel Rubinstein de Ronello, explaining that he was a love child of his Russian mother and a Portuguese nobleman. In fact, he had bought a passport in Shanghai for $2,000. His brother was angry enough to try and sue him for defamation of their mother's character. His mother seems to have forgiven him – at least, she was living in his house at the time of his murder.

On Wall Street, Rubinstein proceeded to add to his fortune by what is now known as 'insider trading' – that is, knowing in advance that certain stocks will rise in value and buying heavily. Rubinstein was always happy to pay for information, and when a director of the Brooklyn Manhattan Transit Company told him that the subways were about to be taken over by the city, Rubinstein rewarded him generously – then bought up 40 per cent of the company's shares. The director had told him something else – that the shareholders were to be bought out at $20 a share, but that those who refused to sell could get as much as $148 a share. Understandably, Rubinstein was one of those who refused to sell, and the resulting profits were $800,000. He repeated the manoeuvre when Western Union merged with Postal Telegraph, netting $2,000,000 on that occasion.

In a later deal, he bought heavily into the Panhandle Producing and Refining Company, which made aviation fuel – essential to the war effort. He then spread false information that sent the stock soaring high, and sold his own stock at a lower price – which had the predictable effect of causing Panhandle shares to slump in value. The shareholders sued him for $5,000,000. But like the shareholders of the Chosen Corporation, they found themselves part of an incredibly complex operation which meant they were owned by half a dozen other companies.

Rubinstein was now enjoying the fruits of success. In spite of his pudginess, his squeaky voice and his habit of prodding people with his forefinger as he talked to them, he was attractive to women, and was never satisfied with more than two or three mistresses at a time – sometimes as many as half a dozen. In 1941, he seemed to be turning over a new leaf when he married a New York model called Laurette Kilborn – she apparently accepted his warning that she must put up with his affairs with other women. On the eve of his wedding in 1941, he dined with Roosevelt in the White House, and at the wedding reception in the Shoreham Hotel in Washington, there were nine ambassadors, dozens of senators and congressmen, and a large number of film producers and Wall Street financiers. The marriage lasted for eight years, and ended only when Rubinstein found himself in prison for draft dodging.

This, Serge realized at the beginning of the war, was the main disadvantage of moving to America – he was eligible for service in the army. He bought an aircraft corporation, and claimed that he was essential to the war effort. He indulged in bribery on an impressive scale, offering members of the draft board blocks of shares. When the war finished, Rubinstein was still a civilian.

But the government was now looking for an opportunity to deport him. Finally, it was proved that during the long struggle to keep out of the army, he had made a false statement – declaring that he was supporting six people in 1940 on an income of just over $11,000. In court, he realized that he

was one of the most unpopular men in America. The specta-
tors hissed him, and some of them shouted: 'Shirker!'
Rubinstein glared back and shouted: 'Suckers!' This caused
such an uproar that the judge had to send five people out of
court. Rubinstein was sent to prison for two years.

Back in Wall Street in 1949, he found that the tide had
turned against him. Nobody wanted to have any dealings
with a shark like Serge Rubinstein. He was forced to do
business through agents – the chief one being a Pole called
Stanley T. Stanley, who was an old school friend.

One of his last major deals involved a company called
Stanwell Oil and Gas, based in Toronto. This was controlled
by a promoter named Lee Brooks, who in 1953 showed his
willingness to sell some of his stock.

Stanley T. Stanley decided to swing the deal through a
company called Blair Holding Corporation, and so
approached the president of the corporation, a man called
Virgil Dardi, saying that he had a client who was anxious to
take control of Stanwell. The client was later disclosed as
Norfolk Insurance, registered in Havana, Cuba. It was one of
many of Rubinstein's companies that existed only on paper.

When Stanwell got wind of the fact that Rubinstein was
involved in the deal, Brooks expressed his unwillingness to
have anything to do with the notorious swindler. Stanley T.
Stanley managed to reassure him, and finally a deal was
done.

So far, the deal had been more or less legal – except that the
Blair Corporation had vastly overvalued the stock that it had
put into the deal. (It is not clear how far this was done with
Rubinstein's connivance.) Rubinstein sued Blair for a million
dollars, and forced them out of the deal – which had no doubt
been his aim all along. Stanwell was taken over by a board of
directors that was made up almost entirely of Rubinstein's
allies.

Apparently the next part of the scheme was to use Stanwell

Oil and Gas – part of the flourishing Canadian Oil Industry – to raid another Canadian Company called Trans-Era Oils. But this part of the scheme was never put into operation. Before that could happen, Rubinstein was murdered.

The time of Rubinstein's death was established as about 2 a.m. His mother had heard raised voices from her son's room at about that time and had called down but received no answer. Her eighty-two-year-old sister had seen a mysterious woman wandering around the hall in the early hours of the morning, but further investigation revealed that the woman was actually the butler checking the doors in his dressing-gown.

It was clear that the motive was not robbery – although Rubinstein's wallet was missing, dozens of other valuable items, including jewellery, had been left untouched.

The police found 2,000 names in Rubinstein's address books, and checked up on every one of them – without result. There were some fingerprints on the masking tape that covered Rubinstein's mouth, but they were not in the police records.

A few months before he was killed, Rubinstein had been beaten up by two men in the street. He claimed that he could not identify them. A few days later, a rock wrapped in a threatening message was thrown through his window. Later, three men were arrested on a charge of making a half million dollar extortion attempt on Rubinstein. One of them was indicted, but was out on bail – on the West Coast – at the time of Rubinstein's murder.

The police were told how Rubinstein had been observed chasing a man down the street, and waving a large bundle of money at him. The man ran into a phone booth and Rubinstein hurled the bills after him in a fluttering shower. The story got around that Rubinstein had offered the man a bribe, and had been baffled and enraged when he was refused. The police deduced from this that Rubinstein had good cause to offer someone a large sum of money, but never found out why.

It was the ladies in the case who gained most of the attention of the tabloids. Two weeks before his murder, Rubinstein arrived at a New Year's Eve White Russian Ball at the Ambassador Hotel with no less than seven beautiful girls – a typically flamboyant gesture. He was known to have a large number of mistresses, to whom he handed keys of his Fifth Avenue mansion – changing the locks whenever he changed mistresses. The police were able to trace six keys, but the ladies who owned them were unable to throw any light on the murder.

The last person – apart from the killers – to see Rubinstein alive was a salesgirl called Estelle Gardener; she had been out to dinner with him at an expensive restaurant on East 58th Street. They had left there shortly before one o'clock, and Estelle had agreed to go into Rubinstein's house for a quick nightcap. She stayed half an hour. It seemed that during the course of dinner, Rubinstein had made several phone calls, one of them to a girlfriend named Patricia Wray. When he had left the restaurant, waiters saw two men who had been sitting at a nearby table go out behind them. The restaurant staff thought that they had been observing Rubinstein all evening.

After Estelle Gardener had left at about 1.30, Rubinstein made another phone call to Patricia Wray, and tried to pursuade her to come over. She made some excuse. Then, it seems, his murderers arrived. From the fact that they beat him, it may be inferred that he knew them, and they had some grudge.

Lee Brooks, of the Stanwell Oil Corporation, was a natural suspect, since he was still smarting from the discovery that Rubinstein had virtually swindled him out of his shares. The fact that Brooks had been questioned about the murder of a textile executive called Albert Langford ten years earlier caused the police to redouble their interest. But they were

Murdered millionaire Serge Rubinstein

On a freezing February evening in 1924, Father Hubert Dahme was shot down on the main street of Bridgeport, Connecticut and died instantly. Passers-by saw a dark figure running into an alleyway. Two weeks later, a hitch-hiker was questioned in nearby Norwalk and when a search of his pockets revealed a .32 revolver – the calibre that had killed the priest – the man, an alcoholic ex-soldier named Harold Israel, was taken in for questioning. Under brutal police questioning, he broke down and confessed that he had murdered the priest in a fit of anger and despair.

The young States Attorney named Homer Cummings felt that he had a watertight case. A girl working behind the counter in the hamburger bar where Israel had taken his meals stated that she had seen him walk past the window at about the time of the murder, and had waved to him. So by this time – although Israel had now retracted his confession – there seemed no doubt that the police had the killer.

Yet Cummings was unhappy. Something struck him as oddly wrong. Israel said he was starving, yet possessed a revolver that could be sold for the price of many meals.

When he questioned Israel, and learned that he had been questioned for many hours under blinding lights, he became even more unhappy. Israel's alibi was that he had been in a cinema, yet he could remember virtually nothing of the plot of the film. Cummings tried asking a number of other people who had seen the same film – and they were equally vague about the plot.

Back at the scene of the murder, choosing a bleak evening at about eight o'clock, his assistants re-enacted the crime. The nearest street lamp was fifty yards away, and at that distance the 'murderer' was just a blurred figure. Next they went into the hamburger joint to talk to the waitress. The first thing Cummings noticed was that the window was covered with a layer of condensation – inevitable on a cold evening. He asked the girl to identify his assistants as they walked past – she was completely unable to see them. Cummings himself then walked up and down outside – the girl waved at two strangers but failed to identify Cummings. When he learned that she had applied for a reward, Cummings drew his own conclusions.

In court on 27 May 1924, Cummings announced to an astonished court that he was dropping the case. The accused man burst into tears – and his subsequent history demonstrated that his brush with death had jarred him out of his alcoholism – he married happily and became a prosperous timber merchant.

Cummings's decision not to prosecute, far from damaging his career, made him something of a celebrity, and he later became Roosevelt's youngest ever Attorney-General.

But the mystery of who did murder Father Dahme is still unsolved.

Murders

unable to establish any connection between Lee Brooks and the death of Serge Rubinstein.

In February 1955, an informer in jail told the police that he thought the death of Rubinstein had occurred as a result of a kidnap plot. His information led the police to a gangster named Herman Scholz who worked as a chauffeur. In Scholz's house in Queens the police found an arsenal of weapons, and a complete set of press cuttings about the death of Rubinstein, as well as curtain cord and adhesive tape of the same type that had been used to tie Rubinstein. Scholz readily agreed that he had planned to kidnap Rubinstein, but that was two years ago, and although he had since renewed his interest in the project, he had a good alibi for the evening of the murder. Finally, the police were forced to let him go. One police theory was that other members of the underworld had stolen the idea from Scholz, but that Rubinstein had died in the struggle. That hardly seemed to explain the fact that he had been badly beaten. And the fact that he was strangled did not seem to be an accident.

There was another surprise for the financial community when his estate was valued at a mere million dollars. Those who knew him well confidently assessed it at least ten times that sum. What had happened to the other nine million? Or had it ever existed? If not, it demonstrates that Rubinstein was also one of the biggest bluffers in the history of modern finance.

Chapter Eleven

The Zodiac Mystery

It is appropriate that the last chapter of this book should also be the strangest story in it.

Between 20 December 1968 and 11 October 1969, an unknown serial killer, who signed his letters to the police 'Zodiac', committed five known murders and seriously wounded two more victims.

On the chilly, moonlit night of 20 December 1968, a station wagon with two teenage lovers was parked in the Vallejo hills overlooking San Francisco. Neither David Farraday nor his girlfriend Bettilou Jensen paid any attention to the white car that drew up and parked about ten feet away. They were jerked out of their absorption by the sound of an exploding gun; as shattered glass from the rear window sprayed into the car, and another bullet ploughed into the bodywork, the girl flung open the passenger door and scrambled out. The boy was following her when the gunman leaned in through the driver's window and shot him in the head. David Farraday slumped across the seat. As the girl ran away, screaming, the man ran after her and fired five times. Bettilou Jensen collapsed before she'd run thirty feet. The gunman then calmly climbed back into his car and drove away.

Five minutes later, another car drove past the open space by the pumping station where the two teenagers lay. Its woman driver saw Bettilou sprawled on the ground, but she did not stop. Instead she accelerated on towards the next town – Benica – and when she saw the flashing blue light of a police car coming towards her, she frantically blinked her own lights to attract its attention. When, three minutes later, the two officers arrived at the pumping station, they found that David Farraday was still alive, but Bettilou was dead. David Farraday died shortly after his arrival in hospital.

The case was baffling. The boy's wallet was intact; the girl had not been sexually assaulted. An investigation into the background of the teenage lovers ruled out the theory that some irate rival had shot them; they were ordinary students whose lives were an open book.

On 4 July 1969, the unknown psychopath went hunting again. In a car park only two miles from the place where the teenagers were shot, a twenty-two-year-old waitress named Darlene Ferrin was sitting in a car with her boyfriend, Mike Mageau. Neither paid much attention when, not long before midnight, a white car pulled alongside them; there were several other cars in the park. The car drove away after a few minutes then returned and parked on the other side. Suddenly, a powerful light shone in on them. Assuming it was a police spotlight, Mike Mageau reached for his driver's licence. There was an explosion of gunfire and Darlene collapsed. Moments later, a bullet tore into Mike Mageau's neck. The man turned and walked back to his own car, paused to fire another four shots at them; then drove off so fast he left a smell of burning rubber.

A few minutes later, the switchboard operator at the Vallejo police headquarters received a call; a man's voice told her that he wanted to report a murder on Columbus Parkway. 'You'll find the kids in a brown car. They're shot with a 9 mm Luger: I also killed those kids last year. Goodbye.'

When the police arrived at Blue Rock Park, they discovered that the caller had been mistaken in one particular: it was not a double murder. Mike Mageau was still alive, although the bullet had passed through his tongue, preventing him from speaking.

This time at least there were a couple of leads. Four months earlier, Darlene Ferrin's babysitter had been curious about a white car parked outside her apartment. When she asked Darlene about it, the waitress replied: 'He's checking up on me again. He doesn't want anyone to know what I saw him do. I saw him murder someone.' She was able to offer a description of the man – round face, with brown wavy hair, probably middle-aged. When Mike Mageau recovered enough to talk, he described the killer as round-faced with wavy brown hair.

A month later, on 1 August 1969, three local newspapers received hand-printed letters which began: 'Dear Editor, this is the murderer of the two teenagers last Christmas at Lake Herman & the girl on 4th of July...' It went on to give details of the ammunition which left no doubt that the writer was the killer. Each letter also contained a third of a sheet of paper with a message in cipher – the writer claimed it gave his name. Each letter contained a different third. He asked that it should be printed on the front page of the newspapers, and threatened that if this was not done, he would go on a killing rampage 'killing lone people in the night'. The letters were signed with the symbol of a cross inside a circle: it looked ominously like a gunsight.

All three letters were published – at least in part and the text of the cryptograms were published in full. Code experts at the Mare Island Naval Yard tried to crack it – without success. But one man – a schoolteacher from Salinas named Dale Harden – had the inspired idea of looking for groups of signs that might fit the word 'kill'.

In ten hours Harden and his wife had decoded the letter. In it the Zodiac said that he preferred killing people to animals because it was so much more fun. He also bragged that he had already killed five people in the San Francisco Bay area. The writer went on to say that when he was reborn in paradise, his victims would then attend him as his slaves.

As a result of the publication of the letter, the police received more than 1,000 tips; none of these led anywhere.

Murders

But another letter to a newspaper began with the words: 'Dear Editor, this is Zodiac speaking . . .' And went on to offer more facts about the Darlene Ferrin murder that left no doubt he was the killer.

Two months later, on 27 September 1969, a young couple went for a picnic on the shores of Lake Berryessa, thirteen miles north of Vallejo. They were Bryan Hartnell, twenty, and Cecelia Ann Shepard, twenty-two, and both were students at nearby Pacific Union College, a Seventh Day Adventist Institution. They had been lying on a blanket in the warm September sunlight, kissing; then they had eaten their picnic.

At about 4.30, both noticed a man across the clearing; he seemed stockily built and had brown hair. The man vanished into a grove of trees. Minutes later, he emerged again, wearing some kind of mask, and carrying a gun. As he came closer, they saw he had a white symbol on the front of the material that hung down from the hood – a circle with a cross inside it.

'I want your money and your car keys,' said the soft voice inside the hood. Hartnell said he was welcome to the seventy-six cents he had. The man began to talk in a rambling way, explaining that he was an escaped convict.

He finally explained that he had to tie them up and produced a length of clothes line; he ordered Cecelia to tie up Hartnell. Then the hooded man tied up Cecelia. They talked for several more minutes, then the man announced: I'm going to have to stab you people.' 'Please stab me first,' said Hartnell, 'I couldn't bear to see her stabbed.' 'I'll do just that,' said the man calmly. He dropped to his knees and plunged a hunting-knife seven times into Hartnell's back. Sick and dizzy with pain, Hartnell then watched him attack Cecelia. After the first stab, the killer seemed to go berserk. He stabbed her five times in the chest, then turned her over and stabbed her five more times in the back. When she finally lay still, the man walked over to their car, drew something on the door with a felt-tipped pen, then walked away.

A fisherman who had heard their screams found them soon after. They were both alive when the Napa police arrived. They had been alerted by an anonymous telephone call. A man with a gruff voice had told them: 'I want to report a double murder', and gave the precise location of the 'bodies'. He left the phone dangling.

Cecelia Shepard died two days later without recovering from her coma. But Bryan Hartnell recovered slowly and was able to describe their attacker. The police had already guessed his identity. The sign on the door of their car was a circle with a cross in it.

This time, at least, the police seemed to have a promising clue. The dangling telephone had been located within six blocks of the Napa Police Department, and it held three fingerprints. But a check with records was disappointing: they were not on file.

Two weeks later, on Saturday, 11 October 1969, a fourteen-year-old girl looking out of a window at the intersection of Washington and Cherry Streets, San Francisco, realized she was watching a crime in progress. A stocky man was sitting in the front of a cab across the street, searching the driver. Then the man got out, leaving the driver slumped across the seat, and began wiping the door with a cloth. Then he turned and calmly walked off northwards.

The girl had called her brothers over to see what was happening. As the man walked off, they rang the police department. Unfortunately, the operator who logged the call just before 10 p.m. made one mistake: she described the assailant as a Negro male adult – NMA. The police patrolman who actually passed the stocky man a few minutes later, and asked him if he'd seen anything unusual, allowed him to go.

The police who arrived at the crime scene found the taxi driver, twenty-nine-year-old Paul Stine, dead from a gunshot wound in the head. The motive seemed to have been robbery. Three days later, the *San Francisco Chronicle* received another Zodiac letter. 'I am the murderer of the taxi driver by Washington Street and Maple Street last night, to prove this here is a bloodstained piece of his shirt. I am the same man who did in the people in the North Bay area.' The letter went on to jeer at the police for failing to catch him, and concluded: 'Schoolchildren make nice targets. I think I shall wipe out a school bus some morning. Just shoot out the tyres then pick off all the kiddies as they come bouncing out.' It was signed with a cross in a circle.

The bloodstained piece of cloth proved to be from Paul Stine's shirt tail. The bullet that killed Stine was reported to be from the same .22 that had killed David Farraday and Bettilou Jensen; in fact, it was a .38.

Despite the threats, the murder of Paul Stine was Zodiac's last officially recorded crime. Yet his taste for publicity seemed to be unsated. At 2 a.m. on 22 October, eleven days after the murder of Paul Stine, an operator of the Oakland Police Department heard a gruff voice telling her: 'This is Zodiac speaking...' He went on: 'I want to get in touch with F. Lee Bailey... If you can't come up with Bailey I'll settle for Mel Belli... I want one or the other to appear on the channel seven talk show. I'll make contact by telephone.' The men he referred to were America's two most famous criminal lawyers.

The only one of the two who was available at short notice was Melvin Belli. 'He agreed to appear on the Jim Dunbar TV talk show at 6.30 that morning. By that time, the news had spread and people all over the bay area were up early to watch it.

At 7.20, a young-sounding caller told Belli that he was Zodiac, but said that he preferred to be called Sam. 'I'm sick. I have headaches.' Bryan Hartnell and the two telephone operators who had actually talked with Zodiac shook their heads; this voice was too young. The caller was eventually traced to the Napa State Hospital and proved to be a mental patient.

Zodiac, meanwhile, kept up his correspondence. In one letter he claimed that he had now killed seven people, two more than Zodiac was known to have killed. And at Christmas, Melvin Belli received a card that began: 'Dear Melvin, this is Zodiac speaking. I wish you a merry Christmas. The one thing I ask of you is this, please help me . . . I'm afraid I will lose control and take my ninth and possibly tenth victim.' Another piece of Paul Stine's bloodstained shirt was enclosed for identification. Handwriting experts who studied the letter confirmed that the writer's mental state seemed to be deteriorating.

Zodiac's correspondence continued. On 24 July 1970, he wrote a letter in which he spoke of 'the Woemen and her baby that I gave a rather interesting ride for a couple of howers one evening a few months back that ended in my burning her car where I found them'. The 'Woemen' that he was referring to was Kathleen Johns, of Vallejo. On the evening of 17 March 1970, a white Chevrolet had pulled alongside her car, and the driver shouted that her rear wheel was wobbling. When she finally pulled in, a 'clean-shaven and neatly dressed man' offered to tighten her rear wheel. But when he had 'fixed' it, and she set off again the rear wheel had spun off. The stranger offered her a ride to a nearby service station. When the man drove straight past it, she realized she was in trouble. 'You know I'm going to kill you?' he said in an oddly calm voice.

Fortunately, she kept her head. When the man accidentally drove onto a freeway ramp, she jumped out and ran, her baby in her arms. As she hid in an irrigation ditch, the man searched for her with a torch. At this point, an approaching truck caught the man in its headlights, and he ran for his car and drove off at top speed. An hour later, as she told her story in a police station, Kathleen Johns looked up at a wanted poster and recognized Zodiac in the composite portrait as her abductor.

When her car was found, it had been burned out; Zodiac had returned and set it alight.

Kathleen Johns had been able to observe Zodiac at close quarters for a longer time than anyone else. Yet even with this new lead, police found themselves unable to trace him.

Since that time, the police have received a number of Zodiac letters, a few of which have been authenticated, threatening more murders. But most policemen in the bay area take the view that Zodiac is dead, or that he is in prison outside the state for another crime. But what seems far more probable is that Zodiac decided to quit before his incredible run of luck came to an end.

But the story of Zodiac is by no means at an end. Its latest chapter is perhaps the most bizarre so far.

In December 1980, Gareth Penn, a California writer with an interest in cryptography, was told by his father – who worked in the Attorney-General's Office in Sacramento – about a Zodiac letter that had not been publicized. In this one, which included a cypher of thirty-two characters, he suggested that 'something interesting' would be found if the authorities were to place a radian on Mount Diablo, a prominent landmark in the San Francisco bay area. A month later, another Zodiac letter said: 'PS: the Mount Diablo Code concerns radians & # along the radians.'

It struck Gareth Penn that, for a man whose letters often suggested that he was little more than a moron, Zodiac must be fairly intelligent to talk about radians.

A radian is an angle which is frequently used by engineers. The simplest way to explain it is as follows: picture a circle, whose radius is made of a piece of black sticking tape. Now take this black sticking tape, and stick it on the outside of the circle. Now it covers an arc whose length is exactly the same as that of the radius. Now draw two lines from the ends of this arc to the centre of the circle. The angle in the centre of the circle – which is 57 degrees, 17 minutes and 44 seconds – is a radian.

Penn was curious about this suggestion. So he went out and bought himself a piece of clear acetate and a marking pen. On the acetate, he drew the angle of a radian. He then laid the acetate on a map of the San Francisco bay area, with the point of the radian on Mount Diablo. He then rotated it slowly, to see what would happen. When the upper arm of the radian passed through the site where Darlene Ferrin and Michael Mageau had been shot, he felt 'as if a ton of bricks had fallen' on him. For the lower arm of the radian passed neatly through the spot on the Presidio Heights where the last victim, taxi driver Paul Stine, had been shot.

He suddenly realized why the last victim was so completely different from the other six. Zodiac had *wanted* to kill someone at that particular spot in the Presidio (an area of parkland given over to the military): because it would fall on the lower line of his radian. In other words, Zodiac was killing with some purely geometrical plan in mind.

In a book called *Times 17*, in which he describes these experiences, Penn writes: 'I don't believe in psychic phenomena, but I suspect that there are subjective experiences which give the impression of ESP. I had one that evening. All of a sudden, there was no sound. Other people were talking in the next room, but I couldn't hear them. The children stopped making noise with their new Christmas toys. The clock stopped ticking. The blackness of the night outside the windows congealed into a sluggish liquid that seemed to ooze through the glass, slowly filling up the room; it was frigid; the cold was not uncomfortable – it was just there.

'I was transported into someone else's head, someone whose evil I could sense the way I could sense the coldness of the black ooze that filled the room. I was looking out through his eyes, but I didn't know where I was or what I was seeing.

All I knew was that I felt utterly dirty. I was disgusted and fascinated at the same time. What an incredible feeling he must have had, to have this knowledge all to himself all these years! Can you imagine what it must feel like to be the sole knower of such a secret?

'It wasn't just that he was a murderer. It was that he had made an orderly, intellectual design appear to be the product of lunacy, and no one had recognized it for what it was – that was his biggest secret. He had had it all to himself until now, and I was sharing it with him. I had the eeriest feeling, one which I still have six years later, of being one of only two people on this planet.'

Naturally, his first action was to go to the police. Captain Ken Narlow, the only original Zodiac investigator still on the job, was certainly interested in this discovery, and so was the *San Francisco Chronicle*. Penn asked the *Chronicle* to make quite sure that they did not mention his name if they used this information. He didn't want his family to become a target for the Zodiac killer.

He told the *Chronicle* reporter something he had noticed and that the reporter said he had noticed too: all the places where Zodiac had murdered people were connected with water. The first two victims had been parked near a water pumping works. The next two had been murdered near Blue Rocks Springs. The next two had been stabbed close to a lake. And the taxi driver's cab had been left parked next to a fire hydrant.

Penn discovered an interesting thing about this last murder. The murder weapon had been a .38. In his trip-book, Paul Stine had made a note saying that he was to take his passenger to the corner of Maple and Washington. In fact, the cab was found a block away, by the fire hydrant, at Cherry and Washington In the letter in which he admitted murdering Paul Stine, Zodiac had stated that the place was Maple and Washington – as Stine had written.

Penn went to the scene, to see if he could understand the contradiction. Then he realized that the block between Maple and Cherry on Washington Street is the 3800 block – that is to say, every house number in that block begins with 38. Zodiac had shot Paul Stine with a .38. Yet he had asked him to stop his taxi a block further on – by a fire hydrant. Again, Zodiac was playing his peculiar and obsessive mathematical game.

In that case, what was the significance of water in the 'cipher'? Was it possible that Zodiac's name was Waters, or Goldwasser, or Dellacqua?

There was another, even simpler possibility. The formula for water is H_2O. The simple way to write this would obviously be HOH. Could this be the initials of the murderer?

A new lead was suggested by one of his friends. The construction of gigantic geometrical figures on the landscape, like the Nazca lines in Peru, or the Cerne Giant in England, is known as Earthform Art. Zodiac's gigantic radian with its apex at Mount Diablo suggested that Zodiac himself might be interested in Earthform Art. This seemed to be confirmed by the fact that one of his communications was on a postcard whose stamp showed a view of the earth from space taken by Apollo 9.

In the Napa library, Penn consulted a biographical directory of artists. What he was looking for was a sculptor whose initials were HOH. He went through the Hs first, looking for someone with a name like Habakkuk Oliver Henderson. He found only one name listed that fitted the initials. And it advised him to look under another name in the dictionary.

Now at this point it must be explained that Gareth Penn actually names the person he is speaking about. And in his book, *Times 17*, he goes on to accuse that person of being Zodiac. His book was privately printed in 1987 and is certainly known to the man whom we shall call HOH. In writing about him in this way, Penn was almost inviting a suit for libel and defamation of character. Yet the person he names has ignored the book – so that now, under the Statute of Limitations, it is no longer possible for him to take legal action. For obvious reasons, I shall continue to refer to his suspect simply as HOH.

Penn turned to the cross reference elsewhere in the dictionary. What he found was an account of a Jewish sculptress who was born in 1907, and was therefore in any case too old to be the Zodiac killer, but the entry mentioned that she had married in 1938, and had one son – whose initials were HOH.

Now admittedly, all this sounds so absurd that it is difficult to take it seriously – rather like the cranks who attempt to prove that the plays of Shakespeare were written by Francis Bacon by digging out complicated ciphers from the Shakespeare plays and poems. It will be up to the reader to decide whether Gareth Penn is a wild crank, whose obsession with cryptography has led him to accuse an innocent man. But first, we need to tell the rest of the story.

What Penn demonstrates very convincingly is that Zodiac has a mind very like his own – obsessed by cryptographs (Gareth Penn is a member of MENSA, an organisation whose members – in terms of IQ – are among the top 2 per cent of the population.) The result is that much of his long book is concerned with numbers and codes. To discuss even half of these would be quite impossible. What follows is simply intended as a brief sample, to give the reader a taste of Penn's method of argument.

Penn quickly noticed that Zodiac seemed to be obsessed by the word 'time'. He also noticed that on the map which had accompanied the Mount Diablo letter, Zodiac had written a series of numbers corresponding to those on a clock face. On the letter to Melvin Belli, there was a message: 'Mail early in the day', together with a clock face. At the scene of his first crime – of which we shall speak in a moment – Zodiac left behind a man's Timex watch stopped at 12.22. In his letters he harped on the word 'time'. One extract read: 'When we were away from the library walking, I said it was about time. She asked me: "About time for what?" I said it was about time for her to die.' In a letter to the *Examiner* Zodiac talked of his killings as 'good times'. Then he asked if the police were having a 'good time' with his cipher. His favourite correspondent was the *Chronicle* – meaning a record of time.

A letter that came to be called 'The Confession' was addressed to the *'Daily Enterprise,* Riverside, Calif, Attn: crime'.

Noting that the name of the paper is not the *Daily Enterprise* but the *Riverside Press-Enterprise* and that the newspaper has no crime department, Penn observes that the address contains precisely thirty-eight letters. The first sentence of his early cryptogram letter is: 'I like killing people because it is so much fun.' Again thirty-eight letters. Zodiac had, of course, killed the taxi driver with a .38.

The letter to Melvin Belli was addressed to '228 MTGY' – an abbreviation for Montgomery. But Belli did not live at 228, but at 722. Penn observes that the number 722 and 228 have something in common – both are exact multiples of 38.

Penn found himself wondering how someone who wanted to express ideas – or names – in numbers would translate letters into figures. One obvious way would simply be to number the letters of the alphabet, so that A was one, B was two, and so on. Another way would be morse code. And the obvious way of writing morse code would be to use Os for the dots and Is for the dashes. Penn tried writing the word 'time' in this code, and then calculated that, as a binary number (binary code, of course, uses only Os and Is) it added up to 38. One of the few letters that had a return address simply had the letters 'R.P.' in morse code. Again, these add up to 38.

When Gareth Penn succeeded in getting hold of a biographical summary of his suspect HOH, he discovered that he had been at a well-known east coast university. He had majored in architecture, and his extra-curricular activities included editorship of a magazine whose title included the number 38. (He also proved to be a member of the Harvard Rifle Team.)

Zodiac also seemed to attach some importance to the number 17. A letter to the *Los Angeles Times* ends with the figure '17+'. One of his letters to the *Chronicle* has a code 'Fk. I'm crackproof'. F is the sixth letter of the alphabet and K is the eleventh, and together they add up to 17.

But what does 'times' and '17' mean? Penn wrote out the phrase 'times 17' in morse code – using Os and Is. The figure he obtained was 9745. In American chronology, this could be read as 7 September 1945. He suddenly recalled that HOH's mother had been born in Poland on 7 September 1907. On 7 September 1945, she had celebrated her thirty-eighth birthday. Penn came to the conclusion that 'times 17' is a disguised form of her thirty-eighth birthday. These two figures would seem to explain Zodiac's curious obsession with 17 and 38.

The total number of stab wounds inflicted on Bryan Hartnell and Cecelia Shepard add up to 17.

This murder differs from the others in many respects. This is the only murder in which Zodiac wore a hood over his head, with his sign, the cross in the circle, inscribed on it.

The day of this murder was the twenty-sixth birthday of Penn's suspect HOH. At that date, his age in days was precisely 9745 – the date at which his mother was thirty-eight.

Although the police and the *Chronicle* soon lost interest in Penn's Zodiac researches – no doubt feeling that all this was little more than a game with numbers – many other people were interested.

Penn admits that he had one major problem. His suspect still lived on the east coast, in the city where he had been to university. The east coast is 3,000 miles away from the west coast of America. So it seemed highly unlikely that the San Francisco Zodiac killer lived on the east coast. Penn admits: 'If it turned out that he didn't look like the Zodiac, write like the Zodiac, or have a history of travel to California during the Zodiac episode, then it was high time for me to stick my head in a bucket of cold water.'

And at this point the *San Francisco Chronicle* revealed Penn's identity. A reporter named Bill Wallace described the discovery of the radian design on the map, and said that it had been advanced by Gareth Penn, a resident of Napa County.

Penn angrily rang the *Chronicle,* and was told that he was paranoid to be so worried. Apart from that, he was not able to get any kind of apology – or even explanation – out of the *Chronicle.*

Five days later, Penn was sitting up late, reading. At exactly half past one in the morning, the phone rang. When he picked it up, there was merely a dialling tone. Moments later, the phone rang again. Again, just a dialling tone. 'I didn't need to speak to the caller to know who it was,' Penn records.

In fact, Penn had been rash enough to drop some postcards – hinting at his discoveries – to his suspect's address on the east coast. They would be franked with the Napa County postmark. Now his suspect knew exactly who he was.

Soon after, he was told that his suspect had complained to the FBI about the postcards. Penn was summoned to the FBI office in San Francisco. The official told him that they had received a complaint about 'what might be construed as extortionate communications'. Had Penn ever demanded money from his suspect?

Penn explained his reasons for believing that HOH was the Zodiac killer. The official told him that they did not believe this could be so, because they had psychological profiles that said so. HOH had a Ph.D., had taught for seven years at another major educational institution, and was now a Cabinet-level official in the Government Office State. He was married – and psychological profiles said that serial killers did not marry. (Penn was later able to list a number of serial killers who were married.)

Penn and the FBI parted on good terms. Penn sent them his material on his suspect, but heard no more.

On 22 June 1981, his phone rang again at exactly 1.30 p.m. The caller asked: 'Is Jim there?' Penn said no, he must have the wrong number. At three in the morning, Penn looked out of his window, and saw that the whole eastern side of the mountains around the Napa Valley were in flames. Subsequently, aeroplanes came and discharged water onto the fire.

At exactly 1.30 a.m., his phone rang again, and again the voice asked: 'Is Jim there?' When Penn said he had the wrong number, the caller said: 'Oh,' and hung up.

Later, it was discovered that the fire had been started deliberately by an unknown arsonist, who had planted a string of bombs. There were nine altogether, containing timers. The timers had been set to go off at 1.30 p.m.

Understandably, Penn felt that whoever had set the bombs to go off at 1.30 was also the individual who had been calling him up so persistently at exactly 1.30.

All this still left the major objection: Penn's suspect lived on the east coast, and the Zodiac murders took place on the west coast. He persuaded a friend to call up his suspect's ex-wife, on the pretext of doing a credit check. He managed to learn from her that her husband had been commuting regularly to California in late 1969 – the period of the Zodiac murders.

Immediately after this phone call, HOH himself rang the friend back, said that he did not have to go to his wife to get details about his career, and offered to send him a CV which would fill in the details of his life. In fact, when this résumé arrived, it claimed that the job that took him to California ended in 1968. Penn was able to disprove this by getting hold of some papers written by his suspect as late as 1970 in which he claimed that he was still working for this firm.

One of the Zodiac postcards of 1971 was an artist's drawing of a condominium project on the east shore of Lake Tahoe, Nevada – within easy reach of California. Penn now learned that his suspect had been working on this project at the time of the postcard.

Penn's collaborator managed to get hold of photographs of the suspect, and some handwriting samples. The handwriting was strikingly similar to that of Zodiac – in *Times 17* Penn prints several pages, comparing the two. Similarities are certainly striking. And the picture of the suspect was also strikingly similar to the composite picture of the Zodiac drawn from the descriptions of those who had seen him face to face.

Penn is convinced that Zodiac committed two more murders, apart from those with which he credited himself. On 30 October 1966, a girl called Cheri Jo Bates drove up to the Riverside City College library, and parked her VW Beetle outside. When she came out, it would not start. A man approached her and offered her a lift. She accepted. On the pretext of walking her to where his car was parked, he lured her three blocks away into an alley where he struggled briefly with her, pinned her to the ground, and cut her throat from ear to ear. He left a Timex watch, set at 12.22 at the side of the body. The wristband was broken, so it looked as if it had come off accidentally during the struggle. A month later, he sent the letter now labelled 'The Confession' to the *Press-Enterprise* that said: 'Miss Bates was stupid. She went to the slaughter like a lamb.' Five months later, another letter was sent in triplicate to the same newspaper, the police and the girl's father. It read: 'Bates had to die. There will be more.' The copy addressed to Cheri Jo Bates's father was signed 'Z'. But the Z was made to look a little like the Arabic numeral 3.

Penn turned the name 'Bates' into morse code, and found that it added up to 1072. Then he turned the word 'death' into morse code – it also added up to 1072. This seemed to be what the writer meant by 'Bates had to die'. Her name was death.

A more recent cipher letter, of thirty-two characters, and ending with the Greek letter omega, has led Penn to believe that Zodiac was also responsible for the murder of a twenty-six-year-old Harvard graduate student called Joan Webster, who disappeared from Boston's Logan Airport terminal on 28 November 1981. Penn believes that the Greek letter omega – the last of the alphabet – is intended as an indication that this is the last of the Zodiac murders.

Times 17 is a bewildering and baffling book, yet it is argued with clarity that leaves no doubt that Gareth Penn is a sane and balanced individual whose experiences have convinced him that he has discovered the identity of Zodiac. The main objection to the book is that it involves so much analysis of numbers and ciphers that the average reader will find it totally confusing. Ronald Knox once satirized the 'Shakespeare cipher' enthusiasts in an essay in which, by analysing Tennyson's 'In Memoriam' he was able to prove, by rearranging the letters in some of its most famous lines, that it was actually written by Queen Victoria. So the sceptical reader will certainly be inclined to feel that it is possible to prove almost anything in this way. On the other hand, it seems fairly clear that Penn was not simply imagining it all. It seems clear that, whether his suspect is the Zodiac killer or not, he certainly entered into the spirit of the thing, and began playing a game of intellectual hide and seek with his tormentor. Only one thing is certain: that when Penn writes 'I can guarantee that you will find this book to tell one of the strangest stories that you have ever read', he is telling no more than the unvarnished truth.

Recent developments in this story are as baffling as the story itself.

In 1987, Gareth Penn concluded *Times 17* with this paragraph:

'In publishing the book which you have just read, I have

exposed myself to civil and criminal prosecution, to the possibility of assassination, to harassment, to ridicule and scorn. I have stuck to my guns for six years, and now I am throwing down the glove. I appoint you, gentle reader, to be my jury. You have seen the evidence. You have patiently and indulgently listened to my interpretation of that evidence for whatever it is worth. I leave it to you to decide whether the effort, the expense, and the risk were worth it.'

He is undoubtedly correct in saying that he has exposed himself to civil and criminal prosecution. Anyone who is publicly accused of being a mass murderer has the right to demand damages. Yet his suspect, HOH, has flatly refused to sue, in spite of being invited to do so several times.

In May 1987, a month after *Times 17* was published, Gareth Penn received an invitation from Jerome Maltz, owner of General Broadcasting System in Los Angeles, to appear on no less than seven talk shows. On 29 May Penn appeared on a three-hour talk show hosted by Anthony Hilder. Hilder had the interesting idea of persuading HOH to appear on the talk show in his capacity as an expert on a running dispute involving the City Council. After twenty minutes, Hilder said that he had one last question: was HOH aware of the recent publication of a book by Gareth Penn in which he was accused of having murdered seven innocent people?

HOH declined the invitation to debate with Gareth Penn on the air, but he did answer the question as to why he was not suing Penn for libel. He said that he consulted with his lawyers and was told that he could not sue, because he could not prove that he had been damaged.

Penn knew enough about the law to know that if a libel takes the form of an accusation of committing a crime, no proof of damage is required.

HOH later called up Jerome Maltz, owner of the station, to complain about the underhand way in which he had been induced to appear on the show. Again, he was asked why he was not suing Gareth Penn. He replied that a lawsuit would be useless, and that an injunction would be unenforceable.

Penn took the trouble to consult a number of lawyers. Without exception, he was told that if HOH were to file suit, he could immediately obtain an injunction requiring him not only to cease publishing the book, but to purchase back every copy that had been sold. 'In other words, he could inflict major economic damage on me for nothing more than the cost of his filing fee.' Moreover, if Penn sold a single copy of the book after the injunction had been obtained, he could go to prison.

In a letter to Maltz, HOH explained that one of his fears is that grief-stricken relatives of the Zodiac victims might seek him out for revenge. Penn has commented that the most efficient way of protecting oneself against this kind of thing is to prove the allegation wrong. After all, all that HOH would have to do would be to prove that he was on the east coast for just one of about thirty dates in which Zodiac was clearly on the west coast.

Even stranger, HOH ended his letter by urging Maltz not to 'rush into a retraction'. In short, having been accused on the radio of being a multiple killer, HOH asked Maltz not to make amends.

Two months later, a reporter on the *Boston Herald* called HOH's lawyer to ask for an interview. The lawyer said that he had advised his client not to give interviews. The reporter then called HOH at his summer home. HOH's reply was: 'People write books about bacteria, too, but nobody interviews the bacteria.' He then went on to explain to the reporter that he was not suing Penn because he could not prove that he had been damaged. In fact, the subject of a libel does not have to prove that he has been damaged. If he is accused of a crime, then he has automatically been damaged.

HOH also commented that a lawsuit would be too costly and that the filing fee alone would bankrupt him. In fact, the fee would be well within the range of a tenured academic with two homes.

Pressed further by the reporter, HOH commented: 'Oh, I suppose I could afford to sue him. But I don't have the time, and time is the most valuable thing I've got.'

Penn comments that after reading *Times 17*, most readers would find that statement highly significant.

On 29 October 1987, the *Boston Herald* published a two-page article headlined 'Author targets lecturer in Zodiac case'. The article included a picture of HOH as he was in 1971, and the artist's impression of Zodiac.

The result was two programmes on radio in Boston, including interviews with Gareth Penn. Still HOH declined to take any kind of action.

In April 1990, the Statute of Limitations for a lawsuit expired in California. A week later, the remains of the Boston student Joan Webster were found in Hamilton. Again, a local paper contacted HOH, raising Penn's allegation that HOH had killed Joan Webster and asking why he was not suing. Once again, HOH explained that he could not prove that he had been libelled.

Two years later, the Statute of Limitations in Massachusetts – where HOH lived and taught – also expired.

Penn concludes his update on *Times 17* by raising the question of why HOH continues to refuse to sue him. His conclusion is that, if anything, HOH is pleased to have been identified as Zodiac. An enormous number of serial killers have written letters to the police – they obviously feel some need to speak about their 'achievement'. But the problem of being an unknown serial killer is that public recognition would also mean being arrested and going to prison. There is a sense then in which, according to Penn, HOH has the best of both worlds. He has been publicly identified as Zodiac, yet he's still at liberty.